Mysteries of Honolulu

Mysteries of Honolulu

By Lopaka Kapanui

For my wife.

Table of Contents

KE ALA MEHAMEHA
The Lonely Road

ALAN DERONIO CAREFULLY GUIDED HIS car along the winding Nuʻuanu Pali Drive at two in the morning. The evening of rehearsal at the Blaisdell Concert Hall was long and tedious, so he was eager to go home and shower and head straight to bed. The headlights now flashed on a lone figure of an old woman slowly making her way alongside the road. The massive roots of the old banyan trees which lined the road made it impossible for anyone to walk without nearly being hit by a passing car, especially this late at night.

It was an elderly Hawaiian woman dressed in a purple jogging suit. Her white hair passed her shoulders, and she was barefoot. Alan pulled the car over just ahead of the old woman and quickly exited his vehicle.

"Tutu! Where are you going? Come in my car, and I'll take you home. Where's your shoes? Come tutu…"

The old woman sat in the front seat as Alan secured her seat belt for her. When Alan got back into the car and continued driving up the road, the old Hawaiian woman spoke slowly but firmly.

"My granddaughter and I went for a walk, and she walks too fast. I don't think she knows that she left me behind. I can't catch up with her like this. Can you hurry and catch up to her? She should be on the right side of the road by now, just past I Lana Wai."

Alan was beside himself at how absent-minded this woman's granddaughter was.

"Your granddaughter let you walk out of the house with no shoes on?" he questioned.

"That's not important now," the old woman replied, "You have to hurry!"

The car took the sharp right at the hairpin turn and had just made the left turn as it passed the gates of the private Ilanawai condos. Alan saw a young Hawaiian woman walking on the side of the road dressed in shorts and walking shoes and wearing a windbreaker jacket. It seemed odd to Alan that he immediately thought her style of dress looked to be outdated compared to the revealing exercise wear that most young local women her age would wear for workouts. Her hair was in a ponytail as she walked with purpose.

"There!" the old Hawaiian woman said, "Can you pop your horn and get her attention?"

A second before Alan laid his hand on the horn, a man dressed in dark coveralls emerged from the bushes behind the woman. He raised his hands as if to grab the woman from behind, but he never got the chance. Alan laid on his horn and turned on the highlights. The man turned around and was blinded by the lights from Alan's car. Disoriented, the only thing the man could do was run into the Nuʻuanu forest. The girl had only seen her would-be assailant for a second and let out a scream.

Parking his car, Alan ran out to get the woman off the road. As he walked her back to his vehicle, the woman, although visibly shaken, thanked Alan again and again.

"Don't thank me. Thank your grandmother. She's the one who knew where to find you."

"My grandmother?" the woman was now confused.

"Yes," Alan said, "I picked her up on the side of the road just past the traffic light. She said the two of you were walking, and you walked ahead of her and left her behind. Did you know she wasn't wearing any shoes?"

The woman stopped dead in her tracks now.

"Wait, wait, wait. You picked up my grandmother on the side of the road, and she was the one who told you I was here?"

"Yes, ask her yourself. She's in my car," Alan led the way.

When the two arrived at the spot where the car was parked, it was empty. Now Alan was confused. The old Hawaiian woman was nowhere to be found.

Looking at the woman, he said, "Look, I'm not crazy. I DID pick her up down the road. She had white hair just past her shoulders, and she was wearing a purple jogging suit. She was barefoot, which is why I gave her a ride. She told me that you would be here."

The woman just stood there crying, "My Grandmother died three years ago. She had dementia. She walked out of the house one day and disappeared. Two weeks later, a small group of hunters found her body near the waterfall. She had her favorite purple jogging suit on... and she was barefoot."

Alan's skin began to crawl, "But how can that be? I talked to her. She sat in that chair, here, in my car. She told me where to go and I... I..."

"Can you take me home?" the woman asked, "I have to tell my parents about this. We never got to say goodbye to my grandmother, and maybe this might make them feel better, knowing that she was here."

"She knew... your grandmother knew that guy was hiding and was waiting to attack you. That's why she kept insisting that I hurry and get to this place."

4

Alan suddenly realized just how dark it was on this piece of road. He helped the woman into the car the same way he helped her grandmother. The woman directed him to make a U-turn and head back down the Pali Highway. He eventually took a left turn on La'imi Road, where the woman pointed out a house just to the right as they passed the traffic light.

The house lay hidden behind a wall of towering mock orange hedges. It was a humble home colored in a light brown with windows trimmed with a darker brown color.

As Alan and the young Hawaiian woman walked toward the front door, she said, "The door is open, just go on in. My parents are in the living room. I'll be right behind you; I just have to take my shoes off. They don't like dirt or mud being tracked into the house."

Alan removed his slip-on leather shoes and opened the door. The living room was nearly bare save for a small couch and a recliner. There was no television, and everything was lit by a standing lamp. He noticed that draped over the recliner was a dark windbreaker jacket like the one the young Hawaiian woman was wearing.

"Can we help you?" came a man's voice.

Alan was startled and nearly jumped out of his pants. Standing in the living room now was a middle-aged

Hawaiian couple staring at him. For some reason, they didn't seem surprised by his presence.

"I apologize, but your daughter told me to come inside and that she would be in in a second. She's right outside. My name is Alan."

The couple bowed their heads in a slight greeting, and the husband motioned his hand to the couch.

"Please have a seat."

Taking a place on the couch, Alan noticed that the couple watched him intently.

"Alan," the father asked, "Why did you come here?"

Confused, Alan replied, "If you don't mind, I'll wait until your daughter gets in, and I'll explain everything."

"She may be a while," said the mother, "Perhaps you could explain everything now?"

The father nodded his approval as if giving Alan the sign to continue. Alan went on to explain the night's earlier events in great detail, right down to the moment where their daughter was now outside the door, removing her muddy shoes.

There was no reaction from the couple as Alan relayed their story. They spent the whole time looking at the floor as he recounted everything. The husband turned and disappeared into a room down the hall and returned with something in his hand. It was a picture that looked old and fragile.

Putting his head down again, he handed the frame to Alan and said, "Read this. It should help you understand everything."

It was a newspaper article from 1982 that showed a picture of the old Hawaiian woman he picked up earlier. Her name was Hattie Aeʻa. Hattie wandered away from her home and was found later by a group of hunters next to a nearby waterfall without any shoes or slippers on, just as the young woman said.

"You can take the article out of the frame," said the mother, "There's more."

The 8" x 10" frame came apart easily. Alan could see that the newspaper had been folded in half to fit into the frame. Opening it up, he noticed another article just beneath the one he'd just finished reading. The young woman's picture was there.

Without even thinking, Alan blurted out, "What?"

"Read," said the father.

The article talked about how the young Lisette Aeʻa was distraught over the disappearance of her grandmother. The woman left the house one night without her parents' knowledge. She had gone in search of her Tutu and was last seen by passersby heading up the Nuʻuanu Pali Drive.

Her body was found the next day near Judd Trail. She had been raped and beaten to death. The murderer was found the next day hiding near the water reservoir and was taken into custody. He was wearing Lisette's windbreaker jacket. The murderer, Jack Briskette, was, himself, killed in prison a year later.

Alan was stunned. The Hawaiian couple just sat there and looked at the windbreaker that lay draped over the recliner.

"Every year on this night," the father began, "Someone driving up that road at two in the morning finds my mother walking, and they give her a ride. She always tells them where to find our daughter, and the driver shows up just in time to save our daughter from being killed. Lisette always tells the driver that they have to come here to our house to explain what happened. They do, or at least they try, and they always insist that Lisette, herself, will come in and verify their story. But she can never come inside. She never comes inside even though she says she'll be right behind them."

It was too much for Alan to take and he ran to the front door and opened it. The young woman was standing there, right outside the door. Her windbreaker was gone now. She stood there with her hands rubbing her shoulders, trying to warm herself.

"She's right here!" Alan yelled. He reached out to grab her by the arm and pull her into the house, but his hand passed right through her as if she were nothing but smoke.

Screaming now, Alan retreated to the safety of the living room.

"Mom. Dad. I'm cold. I need my jacket. Please, let me in. Give me my jacket..."

With that, Lisette slowly faded into nothing.

The old couple held on to one another and wept.

"Everyone wants to help. But they shouldn't. If people really want to help," said the Mother, "They should just keep driving and not give my mother-in-law a ride. That way, my daughter's ghost won't be saved, and she can be killed... and she can finally come home to us."

Alan's head was swimming now. He couldn't comprehend what was happening. All he could mutter was an apology.

"Don't help," the father said, "Don't help."

The Hawaiian couple themselves slowly began to dissolve into thin air and were soon gone as if they were never there.

All Alan could do was scream a hearty scream. Thank goodness he was an opera singer, for the whole neighborhood must have heard him.

'AINA HANAU
Land of My Birth

DANIEL MASON WAS ON VACATION at the Koʻolina Resort when he received a phone call from his mother back home in San Pedro. His younger brother, Kenny, had suddenly passed away in his sleep. The doctors determined that his death was the result of natural causes. Otherwise, Kenneth Mason was the picture of health. Like his older brother Daniel, he was a firefighter who was in tip–top shape. Daniel told his wife to start packing their things but, hearing this over the phone, Daniel's mother insisted that he stay and catch their already scheduled flight home from Hawaiʻi.

"There's really nothing you can do right now," Valerie Mason said, "We'll start making the funeral arrangements so that by the time you get back, everything should be in place and ready to go."

"Alright, Ma," Daniel replied.

"I've already called the station to let them know," Valerie continued, "Bobo has arranged for the bagpipes and the Clydesdales. They're polishing up the old Number 5 as we speak. They all wanted to make sure that Kenny gets to where he's going in style."

The torrent of tears came unexpectedly, and Daniel found that he could not hold back his grief.

"It's okay, Danny," Valerie said on the other end of the line, "You can cry, Danny, it's alright. Goodness, when your father was alive, he was like granite. I never witnessed that man shed a tear for all of the thirty years that I was married to him. Then that day of August 1977 came, and that's when John Taylor broke down and cried like a baby."

"What day was that, ma?" Daniel was lost as to the details of that day and year.

"August 16, 1977. That's the day that Elvis Presley died. Remember?"

Now remembering that day with a bit of discomfort, Daniel replied, "Oh yeah, THAT day."

"I was afraid. John Taylor had been my rock for all of my life, and to see your father sobbing like a baby... it was like watching my world fall apart. And here you are, Daniel, sobbing just like your father on that day except, this time, I'm not afraid. I know your father is here with me now, and he's waiting to take Kenny with him."

"Ma..." Daniel said through his tears, "I have to tell you... when Kenny and I were nine and ten years old, and you whooped his butt for breaking grandma's antique vase?"

"Yes, I remember that," His mother replied.

"I did it. I broke that vase, but I forced Kenny to take the blame for it."

"I know Danny. I knew all along."

"But Mom, you knew all this time, and you didn't say anything? Why?" Daniel was confused.

"Well, Daniel, it was either that or me having to tell you that I'm not your mother. And that Dad was not your father and Kenny wasn't your brother. You see, Danny, you're adopted. That's why I never said anything all these years."

There was a long pause on the phone as Daniel tried to take in this newly found revelation.

"Ma," he began, "Are you serious? I'm adopted?"

"No," Valerie said, "Of course not! But that's what you get for telling Kenny he was adopted when he was a kid!"

"Dammit, Ma! Even at a time like this! I didn't even see that one coming!"

"Danny, it's time for you to get off of the phone and enjoy your vacation with Corrine. Mama loves you now and give my love to Corrine too. Bye."

"Bye, Ma. Love you," Hanging up the cell phone, Daniel fell into Corrine's arms and wept, "He's gone, Corrine. Kenny's gone. It was unexpected, and I never got to say goodbye."

Corrine never got to express her sympathies to her husband at that moment because, in a flash, he was back on his cell phone.

"Who are you calling?" Corrine asked.

"Alex."

"Oh, noooo… Daniel! Don't call him! He's an idiot! Ever since he got you hooked on that stupid ghost hunting show, that's all you two talk about!"

"I have to know, Corrine! I wasn't there when Kenny died! I want to know if he's trying to communicate to me or if he's gonna show up here!" Daniel said excitedly.

Yelling at him now, Corrine said, "Why would he show up here, Daniel? He didn't die here! He died in San Pedro in his sleep, in his own bed for chrissakes!"

Completely ignoring Corrine's urgings, Daniel continued the rest of his phone call out on the lanai.

"Hey, Alex?"

"Daniel, what's up?" Alex said.

"Listen, my brother, Kenny, passed away today. He died in his sleep at home."

"Oh man, I'm sorry to hear that, Daniel. Is everything okay? You need anything?"

"No, no, I'm fine. The reason I'm calling is that I think Kenny is going to try and show himself to me or at least try to tell me something. I mean, what would those guys on the show do in a situation like this?" Daniel asked.

"They would start to try and establish communication and then take a bunch of pictures and video," Alex said.

"Yeah, yeah, okay, okay, I better start doing that. Alright, thanks, Alex! I have to go. Corrine's having a cow. I'm on vacation in Honolulu, and I'm not supposed to be on the phone."

"Oh, yeah, sure, sure. Hey, do me a favor? If you get anything on film or any pics, make sure you send me a copy, okay?" Alex asked excitedly

"Sure thing, man. You got it! Talk atcha later!" Alex hung up and went back inside. Corrine was already standing there with a cold stare directed at her husband.

"You're a piece of work, Daniel Mason. Your brother just died, and now you're talking about getting his ghost to communicate with you? That's really morbid. Maybe I should get Alex to fly down here so that the two of you can enjoy OUR vacation together?" Seeing that she wasn't going to get a response from her husband, Corrine turned away in frustration, "Never mind. I'm going for a walk."

With that, she stormed out and slammed the door.

Ten minutes later, Daniel found himself downstairs at the poolside bar. The atmosphere was quiet. There were a few young couples scattered throughout the establishment, utterly oblivious to anything else around them.

The bartender brought Daniel a shot of Kentucky Bourbon and walked over to the far right side of the bar, where he resumed his conversation with a pretty young blonde who was obviously a first–time visitor to the islands. She sat there enraptured with whatever story it was that he was telling her. Of course, stories like that were all designed for one purpose. Daniel shook his head.

"Assholes are the same all over the world," he muttered to himself.

"Would you like another shot, or should I just leave the bottle?" A second bartender appeared and was holding the bottle of Kentucky bourbon just above the shot glass, ready to pour.

"Can you do that?" Daniel asked.

"Well, that depends. Are you a guest at The Koʻolina Resort?" the bartender questioned as he held the bottle away from Daniel.

"Yeah. Eleven–oh–five. Daniel Mason."

Alright. Why don't I just continue to pour, and you tell me what's on your mind? By the way, my name is Kaniala," the bartender reached out and shook Daniel's hand.

"I'm Daniel. Run that name by me again?" he asked.

"Kaniala," the bartender repeated, "It's Hawaiian for Daniel."

"Ah hah hah hah!" Daniel laughed, "Interesting coincidence."

"Here in Hawai'i, there is no such thing as a coincidence. Everything is as it is meant to be," Kaniala said.

"Alright, alright. Let's not get into any of that deep stuff. I'm a meat and potatoes kinda guy, plain and simple. I don't even like fixings on my cheeseburgers or hot dogs. I like things just one way so I can understand stuff a lot better. Any extra garnish just makes things more complicated," Daniel explained.

"I see where you're coming from," Kaniala replied, "Sometimes even ketchup and mustard can mess up a good Polish hot dog."

"Right!" Daniel agreed, "That's why, whenever I'm working on a project of some kind, I do it elsewhere, never in or around my own home. Do you know why?"

"No, sir, I don't."

"Because three things are going to happen if I am doing a project at home. See, I like to restore old furniture. That's my hobby, but I never do any of that at home, and here's why; if I do it at home, number one, at some point, my wife is going to wander into the garage where I'm

16

doing my work, and then number two will happen. First, she'll ask me what I'm doing. Second, I'll explain it to her. Third, she'll take a look at what I'm doing and give me a compliment, and then in the same breath, she'll suggest another way to do it better. The result of all of that becomes number three; I get pissed off, and I chuck the whole project."

Kaniala smiled and poured Daniel another one. Throwing back the bourbon, Daniel leaned forward and asked, "You like that one, huh? See? You get it right?"

"No," Kaniala continued to smile, "You said three things would happen. But actually, six things happened because you quoted three other items within your list of three things, so you actually came out with six."

Looking up for a second, Daniel began to reconfigure the numbers in his head.

"Uh, yeah, you're right! Must be the bourbon!" Daniel laughed.

"But that isn't what's really troubling you?" Kaniala asked.

With his arms folded over on the bar, Daniel leaned closer. "My younger brother died at home today back in San Pedro. That's where I'm from, see? He died in his sleep, my mom said. He wasn't sick or anything like that; he just went in his sleep. My friend back home, his name's

Alex, he got me into watching those ghost hunting shows. And see, it talks a lot about people who die suddenly. I'm thinking that maybe Kenny is trying to communicate with me, or maybe he's just hanging around trying to give me some message, or maybe he wants me to take a picture of him somewhere so that I'll know he's with me. You know?"

The tears surprised Daniel as he began to wipe them away with his hands. Kaniala handed him a few napkins and poured him another shot of bourbon.

"We're both firefighters, me and Kenny. As a matter of fact, I'm the one who got him in. I was always the one who looked out for him and protected him. I guess I kinda forgot at some point that Kenny was already a man himself with a family of his own. I was selfish, see? I felt like Kenny had forgotten about me and that he didn't need me anymore. We got into this argument before I left home to come here on vacation over… over him not pulling his weight at the station. It was stupid because Kenny was doing more than what was expected of him, but I was just being a jackass. We started getting loud and yelling at each other and, pretty soon, I shoved him, and he shoved me back and one more shove from me, and the next thing I knew, I was on my ass! That kid knocked me flat on my ass! I couldn't believe it. My last words to him were, 'I don't have a brother anymore.'

18

"Hey, but I thought that things would blow over and that, once I got home, I'd go see him, and we'd talk and then forget about the whole thing. But today, my mom called to tell me that Kenny died in his sleep, and that's why I need to see him. That's why I hope he'll try to speak to me or something so that I can… so that I can say I'm sorry. I haven't even told my wife about this."

Kaniala poured the bourbon again and began to share something with Daniel.

"Our people have a strong association with the place that they come from. That's what ties them to their families and their genealogy. A sense of place is everything to us. In some instances, the umbilical cord or the afterbirth of a child is buried in the ground with a certain kind of plant or tree on top of it. That action alone physically and spiritually binds that child to the land of his or her birth. We call it 'aina hanau. Even when our elders passed, we would sometimes bury them in the front of the house or even underneath the house. Family was always kept close. They were never taken far away to be buried, as is the custom of today."

Looking at Daniel now, Kaniala continued, "With that tidbit of information, I am going to conclude the pouring of anymore bourbon. I'd like you to make it back to your room while you still have two good wheels to work with."

Daniel agreed, "Good idea. I've had my limit. What's the damage here?"

"No harm, no foul, Mr. Mason. Tonight your money is no good here," Kaniala said.

"I won't hear of it!" Daniel insisted, "Even with all that deep talking you did just now, I still have to leave something for your trouble for having to put up with me!"

Fumbling into his pants pocket, Daniel finally managed to pull out his wallet and handed Kaniala a fifty–dollar bill.

"Here you go. Don't give me a hard time now," Daniel looked up and saw that the bar was empty. There was no one there save for the first bartender, who was still talking to the young, pretty blonde.

"Excuse me! Excuse me!" Daniel was now waving to the first bartender, who seemed mildly irritated.

Walking over to Daniel, he asked, "Yes, sir, how can I help you?"

"What happened to the other bartender that I was just talking to? Kaniala was his name."

The first bartender was openly upset now.

"Sir, you were sitting here talking to yourself for the past hour. There was no one here. And if you're trying to be funny, then I think that what you just said is in poor taste. A lot of people here loved Kaniala and are still upset about what happened!"

20

"What?" Aside from being affected by the bourbon, Daniel was genuinely confused.

"Kaniala was our other night shift bartender. What you said is in really poor taste. It would be cruel if Bryn overheard you."

"Wait. I think we're a little mixed up here. Who are you talking about?"

"Kaniala. He was killed in a car accident earlier today while he was on his way here. You see that woman sitting at the other end of the bar? That's Bryn, Kaniala's girlfriend. She came here tonight to surprise him and tell him that she's four months pregnant with his child. No one's told her yet about Kaniala. No one knows how to break it to her. So, if you're trying to be funny, then you pretty much suck. If there's nothing else, I'll leave you to yourself."

A few minutes later, when Daniel returned to his room, he found Corrine sitting on the queen-sized bed watching a movie. He quickly fell into her arms and apologized and explained the situation with himself and Kenny before they left to come to Hawai'i. He then shared with Corrine his strange experience with the bartender named Kaniala and the conversation they had. At first, Corrine was shocked by what Daniel told her but, after a while, as she thought more about it, she looked at Daniel with a sudden revelation.

"Daniel?" She said.

"We need to go home," he answered.

"Yes!" she replied in amazement, "How did you know that?"

"Because I was just thinking about what the bartender was saying about how Hawaiian people having a strong sense of place..." Daniel began to trail off.

"Oh, my God!" Corrine gasped, "I was thinking the same thing!"

"Let's go home, honey, okay?" Daniel asked.

Corrine couldn't have agreed more.

As soon as Daniel and Corrine arrived at the airport, they drove straight to Kenny's house. Pulling up to the driveway, Daniel wasn't surprised to find his mother in the front driveway of Kenny's house with Kenny's wife and children. They were all visibly upset and shaken. His mom had just arrived at Kenny's house minutes earlier because of Karen's hysterical phone call about her husband sitting on the bed in their room. The children saw their father first and then ran out of the room screaming for their mother.

"Daniel, what are you doing home so early?' Valerie asked.

"I'll explain everything, Mom!" Corrine said as she got out of the car, "Daniel needs to talk to Kenny."

"Talk to Kenny? Wha... what's going on?" Valerie was dumbfounded.

Rushing through the living room and then the kitchen, Daniel took an immediate left into Kenny's bedroom and found it empty. His disappointment only lasted for a second when he heard his name called from behind him.

"Danny?"

Daniel turned around so quickly that he almost lost his balance. His heart skipped a beat as he saw Kenny standing in front of his closet.

"Danny," Kenny said.

"Ken," nearly speechless, Daniel continued, "How come you're not transparent? I can still see you like you're flesh and blood."

"I don't know," Kenny said, "All I know is I can't go because I have to finish something."

Daniel was even more dumbfounded as he asked the next question, "How are you doing that?"

"Doing what?" Kenny answered.

"Your mouth isn't moving, but I can hear you talking to me in my head!"

"I don't know."

"Kenny, I'm sorry for what happened before I left. I was just hurt and afraid that... that you didn't need me anymore," Daniel cried, "I was always your big brother, and I got used to you needing me. Once you got married and had a family, that all changed. I was selfish, Kenny, and I'm so sorry. I love you so much, man, and I miss you."

Breaking down now, Daniel found it hard to continue.

"That's it," Kenny said, "That's what I'm supposed to do. I'm supposed to tell you that it's all okay. I already forgave you, Dan, and I'll always love you. You'll always be my big brother, but I need to tell you that you have to forgive yourself. What happened to me wasn't your fault. It was just my time. That's all. Can you do that for me, Dan? Can you forgive yourself?"

Daniel could only nod in response.

"Hey, you guys," Kenny said suddenly.

Daniel saw Kenny looking off to his side. He turned around to see Karen and the kids standing at the bedroom door in shock. His mother was beside herself with tears as Corrine held her by her shoulders.

"Daddy?" Kenny's daughter, Grace, asked, "Do you still love us something awful?"

Nodding in reply, everyone heard Kenny in their heads just like Daniel did earlier.

"Awfully," looking at everyone, Kenny continued, "I love you, Karen. You girls, be good to your mom and listen to her, okay?"

Everyone replied, even though the question was meant for his immediate family.

"Mom? Dad's here waiting for me. I have to go, but he says he loves what you've done with the family and that YOU were like granite."

Valerie could only weep at the revelation of what Kenny had just shared. Looking again at Daniel as he began to slowly fade into nothing, Kenny concluded, "Knocked you on your butt."

"Pssshhh!" Daniel said, "That's not gonna happen a second time!"

"It won't," with that, Kenneth Paul Mason was gone.

Everyone hugged each other and held on tight for a few minutes as they all slowly began to absorb the extraordinary event that just took place in front of them.

"Karen," Valerie began, "When did you have a chance to call Daniel and tell him about Kenny's ghost appearing in this bedroom?"

"I didn't, mom. I only called you to come over after it happened, then I was outside in the front driveway with you the whole time. I had no idea that Daniel was even back from his vacation until he drove up in his car!" Karen replied.

"Danny, how did you know?" His mother asked.

"A friend I made in Honolulu told me. His name is Kaniala; it's Hawaiian for Daniel, just like my name. He said that the Hawaiian people have a strong sense of family and place, like the place where they come from or the land where they were born. You see, Alex got me hooked on that ghost hunting show…"

"Oh, Daniel," his mother interrupted, "Shows like that aren't good for you. They'll rot your brain!"

"Maaaaaaaa!" Daniel shouted in frustration.

"Alright!" Valerie conceded, "Go on."

"Anyway, after you told me about Kenny and all, I had this stupid idea that he would try to talk to me from the other side, but Corrine and I got into this disagreement about it. I went down to the pool bar at the resort, and that's where I met Kaniala, the bartender. He's a very wise Hawaiian man who gave me some wisdom even though I didn't know what it was at the time. When I thought about what he told me about Hawaiians having a strong sense of place, that's when I realized that Kenny could never talk to me while I was in Honolulu because that isn't where he died, and that wasn't where he had a sense of place. His place was here, in his own home. That's when I knew I'd find him here. Not in Honolulu. Corrine helped me know that too. That's why we cut our vacation short and came back."

Later that evening, as Corrine finished preparing dinner, Daniel had just come from taking a shower and was beginning to settle into his favorite chair in the living room.

"I'll have dinner out there shortly. I set the channel for your favorite ghost hunting show!" Corrine called out.

"Ah," Daniel grunted, "I don't wanna watch that show anymore. It's all set up, just like wrestling."

Corrine slowly walked out of the kitchen and made her way to where Daniel was seated.

"Did I hear you correctly? Do you have a fever or something? That's your favorite show! Is something wrong?" Daniel's wife was genuinely worried, "And where's Alex? He's usually here by now."

"I told Alex that I'm not interested in watching that show anymore. So, I guess he won't be coming over anytime soon. What a silly show, huh? A person's ghost is connected to the place where they came from," Daniel said, nodding.

"So what are you going to watch now?" Corrine asked.

"Something I think we would both like," Daniel answered, "Hawai'i Five-0."

WAIHO
Leave it Alone

I KA WA KAHIKO, in the days of old, whenever our people traveled, be it from one kulanakauhale to another, they were sure to bring those items with them that would provide for their basic needs of sustenance and comfort. Whether it was a water gourd or a sleeping mat, or even a pillow made of lauhala, these items were a personal, everyday part of life for the maka'ainana. Some of these items were given names and were treated as if they were traveling companions. For moena, sleeping mats that were given names, no one but the owner could use them. When he or she had passed, the moena was burned so that no one else would be able to use it. This is the same practice in hula. Our pahu drums that we make ourselves are given names just as our other handmade hula implements. No one is allowed to use them unless you gave them specific permission.

Such was the case when I was growing up. I cannot speak to the experience of other Hawaiians because every family is unique. It was constantly stressed to us as children that if something did not belong to you, you had no right to touch it unless you had permission from the person to whom it belonged. Otherwise, "Mai hoʻopa. Waiho ia."

The following story is true. It happened during a time when life seemed simpler. Our parents worked hard so that we could have better lives. Mom and pop stores had not yet been wiped out by big-box superstores that offer us an overabundance of what they think we need. We thought marriage lasted a lifetime, and holidays were family-oriented, maintaining their simple sanctity and reverence.

Kekaha is a sleepy, idyllic town on the west end of Kauaʻi that seems to have been suspended in time. Many of the old houses from their heyday as a bustling plantation community still remain. Many of its residents are ʻoʻiwi who migrated from the island of Niʻihau to make a better life for themselves and their issue.

This was Mariesse Tilton's first time on the island of Kauaʻi. The view of the Kekaha neighborhood from the back seat of her cousin's van gave her the impression of time travel. She couldn't help but think that, whatever affected the rest of the world at this very moment, it had left Kekaha out of the loop.

Her parents recommended that she go to Kauaʻi to spend some time with her mother's side of the family and get to know them a bit better. She had only met her cousins, the Balasans, at weddings and funerals. Mariesse's mother began to see how over-worked her daughter had become and thought that a short vacation on Kaua'i would be a good time to relax and re-energize. For someone who went to an all-girl Catholic school, Mariesse's mother was quite the modern-aged, free spirit.

The Balasans were very accommodating and made sure that Mariesse was well taken care of. Each day became an opportunity to visit a new site on the island of Kaua'i or visit other extended family. Finally, in the middle of the second week of her stay, Mariesse decided that she was comfortable enough with the area that she could take a quiet morning stroll on the beach by herself. The time read 9:03am as she strolled along a pretty stretch of sand with a few wisps of long grass here and there. The wind that came in off the water was soothing, and it helped to relieve the bit of heat that came from the sun.

Suddenly, everything went silent. The wind stopped. There was only heat. Mariesse looked around and could see fronds of the coconut trees across the street blowing in the wind. She turned to face the ocean and could see the waves breaking just before the shore. She watched the wind carry the salt spray above the water. But she could hear and feel none of it. It was as if she were suddenly encapsulated. For a moment, the only sound she could hear was that of her breathing becoming more rapid.

Then, somewhere behind her, she heard the voice of a woman humming a tune to herself, which she did not recognize. She turned to her left and saw, not more than fifteen feet away from where she stood, a Hawaiian woman sitting on a large rock that was hidden just beneath the water.

Her back was facing Mariesse, and her hair was long and black. Her skin was tanned to an almost coconut brown color. She was topless from what Mariesse could see, and she was combing her hair back with a short hand–held hair comb. Mariesse watched as the woman now put her hair over the left side of her shoulder and began to pull it forward. That's when the woman noticed her. Mariesse smiled and gave a short wave. The woman looked startled and angry at the same time. In a quick second, the Hawaiian woman dove headfirst from the rock, disappearing into the water in one smooth motion, having never made an effort to stand up to do so.

Just as suddenly as the feeling of being encapsulated happened, it quickly went away. It was almost as if she was standing in a soundproof room, and the door was abruptly ripped away. The heat and wind seemed to blast against her like a tiny explosion. She stood in disbelief for a moment until the wind began to bring tears to her eyes.

Although the entire short event seemed unbelievable, what startled Mariesse the most was that, as the woman dove into the water, she had no legs. She only had a long tail that began at her waist. Mariesse got closer to the rock that the woman was sitting on and saw that she had left her hair comb behind. From what she could tell, it was made of a turtle shell. She decided that she would hold on to it until she saw the Hawaiian woman again.

Mariesse returned every morning of her vacation after that but to no avail. The strange woman with the long tail never returned. Since the day she saw the woman on the beach and found the beautiful turtle shell hair comb, Mariesse became sicker and sicker. She had little or no appetite to eat during the day, and at night she couldn't sleep because of the horrible nightmares. Dark, frightening images of being pulled down into an underwater sea cave and being eaten alive by a terrible, black-colored creature covered in slime. It would call her name in the dream. Whenever Mariesse would answer, the creature would only repeat one word.

"Na'u."

The Balasans were concerned and became distressed when Mariesse didn't answer her phone calls or come to the door. The eldest cousin, Elode, finally expressed his concern about his ʻOʻahu cousin and convinced the property manager o let him into Mariesse's room. Elode almost threw up because the room reeked of rotten fish. He glanced around the darkened room and saw his cousin lying on her bed, hardly breathing. Her skin was pale white and peeling. Her hair was wet and matted about her face. In her hand, she clutched the turtle shell hair comb.

Instead of taking her to a doctor, Elode drove his cousin to the home of the Kanahele family. The man of the house was a deacon in his church, but everyone knew that he was also a powerful Kahuna. Elode frantically knocked at the door of the house, waiting for an answer. The deacon emerged to find the frightened Filipino man on his porch.

"Kanaka! My cousin, she sick! Not hospital kine, dis one! I seen em happen before when I was small! Anyt'ing you can do, help her, please! She stay in my car, sick!" Elode pleaded.

Nodding, the man said softly, "Bring your cousin inside."

After laying her on a couch in a back room, the deacon noticed the turtle shell hair comb that Mariesse held in her hand. The look on the man's face was deadly serious. He tried several times to take the comb from Mariesse, but she literally had a death grip on it. As huge a man as Kanahele was, he could not pry the object from her.

He looked at Elode and said, "You hapai your hoahanau to the van, and we go to the beach."

Without question, Elode carried his cousin into his van, and the three sped off toward the beach at Kekaha. They finally arrived at the very spot where Mariesse had first seen the Hawaiian woman sitting on the rock.

"Now," Kanahele commanded, "Hapai your cousin over here and put her hand on the rock."

Following the kahuna's orders, Elode held his cousin in one hand and placed her hand holding the hair comb on the rock. The second Mariesse's hand was laid on the huge pohaku, it relaxed its grip, and the turtle shell hair comb gently fell and rested on the rock.

"Maika'i," Kanahele said, "Ha'alele now. We go."

However, even before they could leave, a woman's hand came from the other side of the rock just below the spot where the turtle shell hair comb lay. The hand quickly snatched the hair comb up and disappeared. The two men heard a loud splash and saw the Hawaiian woman looking at them from the water not more than a few feet from where they stood. Elode dropped to the sand with his cousin in his arms and prayed for their lives. The deacon fell to both knees and bowed his head in deference to the akua of his ancestors. This was not a mermaid or kananaka. It was a moʻo wahine.

When Mariesse recovered from her sickness a short time later, she would have no recollection of the events that transpired. The family feared that telling her what little they knew would frighten her badly. Instead, they explained that she had fallen into a deep sleep because of food poisoning as the result of eating some spoiled pork gisantes.

LUA

NICOLE KAHOʻOHULI WAS MURDERED ONE night while on her way to attend a class at the University of Hawaiʻi. Her assailants, Gary Catao, Fowler McGuire, and Jermel Evans took her by surprise as she exited her car in the parking structure above Cooke Field. On the contrary, the surprise was on them. Nicole fought back with an animal–like ferocity and nearly overpowered the three men who were twice her size. She was so infuriated at the attempt of these three in trying to rape her that she never called out for help. As far as she was concerned, she was going to kill them all with her bare hands. Fowler McGuire escaped Nicole's fury long enough to run a considerable distance to his car and start it up. He was speeding at nearly 70 miles per hour by the time he returned to the scene of the assault. Nicole already had Jermel Evans prone on the ground after delivering a punishing kick to his groin. All Gary Catao could do now was cover-up as the young woman peppered him with an onslaught of elbow strikes to his skull. In every instance when Gary Catao covered up to protect his head, Nicole would hit him with blinding uppercuts to his ribs.

Fowler McGuire would later tell the police that when he returned to the scene, he witnessed Nicole hurting his friend Gary and then saw that Jermel Evans was on the ground. He thought Jermel was dead and that Nicole had killed him. The sight of his childhood friend lying on the ground, lifeless, infuriated him. He felt that he was left with no choice but to come to Gary Catao's defense, who he was also afraid would be killed by Nicole Kahoʻohuli.

In a split second, Fowler swerved his car toward Nicole and hit her head-on. She died on impact. The three young men panicked and left her there. They thought that they had gotten away with it and that no one would ever find out, but they had two things that were already working against them.

Number one, the entire incident was recorded on a security camera. Exactly where the security guards were during the assault was never determined. Number two, Nicole herself had left significant scratch marks on each of her attackers before she died. Gary Catao was scratched on his neck with deep gouges from Nicole's forefinger and middle finger. Jermel Evans had four scratch marks on his left shoulder, and Fowler McGuire had five small chunks of flesh taken out of the back of his right calf muscle as he tried to escape Nicole's attack.

While the young men were arrested within twenty-four hours and charged with murder. They were released on bail into their parents' custody within a week, courtesy of the best lawyer that Fowler McGuire's wealthy father could afford.

Daylee and Leena Kahoʻohuli were just pulling up to their Kalihi home when they saw their friend Mike Nakamura in his police uniform standing in their driveway. Mike and Daylee were childhood friends from the time they met in a karate class in Waipahu. They got into a fight with each other the first day and, after being severely reprimanded by their sensei by being whacked on the head with a kendo stick, they became life-long friends.

Mike had a serious look on his face, which was usually the look they called his "work face."

"Hey, Mike," Daylee said, "What's up?"

Leena gave Mike a hug and started to walk towards the front door, assuming he wanted to talk to her husband.

"Uh, Leena. You have to hear this too."

Leena turned, serious now, "Mike? Did something happen?"

"Daylee. Leena. I wanted to be the one to tell you, you know, before you found out on the TV or something..." Mike's voice started to crack.

"What is it, Mike? Sounds serious," Daylee said.

Mike drew in a deep breath and let it out, "This isn't easy for anyone, so I'm just gonna say it. It's Nicole. She uh, she was killed last night. Three men tried to assault her, but she fought back. One of them got away and came back with his car. He hit Nicole at full speed. She died on impact. It was so quick... she didn't..."

It only took a few seconds before the reality of Mike's statement hit them. Leena went pale, and her legs began to go out from under her. Daylee and Mike caught her just in time.

"Mike," Daylee asked, "Was that the girl on the news? The one at UH? We just heard it on the radio. Is that the one Mike?"

Daylee's voice wavered now, and his mind did not want to accept what he just heard, "Please, Mike! Please! Tell me it was someone else's daughter, Mike! Please!"

Mike could do nothing but stand there and cry. Leena suddenly stood up and began to beat Mike on the chest, screaming at him the whole time.

"How dare you come here and tell us something like that? What's wrong with you? Are you some kind of sick person? You go get Nicole and bring her home right now, Mike Nakamura, or we will never talk to you again!"

Holding Leena back, Daylee asked Mike once more, "Mike. That couldn't have been Nicole. C'mon now, this is all some bad joke, right? Did you hear what they did to that poor girl? They ran her over for chrissakes! Who would do that to Nicole? Who? This is all some kind of mistaken identity thing? Right, Mike?"

No words came. Only tears.

Daylee screamed at Mike now, "Don't just stand there! Say something! Say something!"

The words would never come. Nicole was dead. Their lives would never be the same.

Nicole's services were difficult for Daylee because he couldn't bring himself to view his daughter's body. He felt that if he didn't, it would mean that somehow Nicole was still alive and that maybe she had gone off to college somewhere far away, like Europe. Leena was able to deal with Nicole's death differently than her husband. Of course, she was devastated and heartbroken, but she knew that her love for her only child would never diminish. The pain was nearly unbearable, but faith told her that she would see her child again.

The services had been going on for twenty minutes, and Nicole's father was nowhere to be found. Daylee stayed outside in the courtyard of the funeral home the whole time. He sat there as he felt his emotions stirring within him. He was suddenly jolted back to reality when he felt a sharp, stinging pain on the back of his neck. Looking up, he saw his father standing over him with his eyes colored blood-red. Daylee knew from experience that this meant his old man was pissed.

"You getchur ass in there right now, and you honor your daughter! This is her funeral services, and you are her father, so move your ass, now!"

Manford Kaho'ohuli was a man that no one ever said no to. He was a broad, big-boned, Hawaiian man who worked as a Stevedore his whole life. The one thing Manford never tolerated was foolishness or idle behavior from a grown man, especially not from his own son.

"I no can, Papa. It's too much for me," Daylee replied.

Manford picked his son up by the scruff of his coat with one hand and stood him upright, "Too much for you? TOO MUCH FOR YOU? You know what is too much, hah? Me having to see you act like one panty!"

"Eh, I not one panty!"

"Boy," Manford was boiling now, "You betta shut your mouth right now before I broke your jaw. You hear me?"

Putting his head down, Daylee replied, "Yes, Papa."

"You t'ink you da only one hurtin'? You no tink I hurtin' or your maddah not hurtin'? Das our only grandchild in that coffin! Everybody who stay hea tonight hurtin'. You go in there, and you honor your daughter and give her your aloha. Oddah wise, she no can go to Kuaihelani to be with her ancestors."

Daylee looked at his father, "Papa? You can take me inside? I need help."

Manford nodded, "I go wit, you boy."

Nicole lay there in her favorite holoku. The one that Daylee brought for her the first time she danced hula for a performance during her senior year at Roosevelt High School. He took her hand and held it in his and quickly noticed that it was cold and stiff. The finality of death had taken his daughter. That was the reality of it. The tears didn't come. There was no overwhelming grief, and he didn't find himself tempted to throw himself on his

41

daughter's coffin once it was lowered into the earth. Instead, there was clarity. When the opportunity had come, Daylee grabbed Mike and pulled him aside.

"Let's talk a walk," Daylee said.

They walked to the top of Mililani cemetery and sat on the bench near the statue of Christ when Mike asked, "What's up?"

"Mike," Daylee continued, "Tell me honestly, not as a police officer but as my friend, do you think that it's right that those three guys get to walk away scot-free?"

"They didn't get away. They're out on bail. But don't worry. They can't fart in this town without us knowing about it."

Shaking his head now, Daylee said, "That's not what I asked you, Mike. Stop thinking cop and just think like a regular, everyday human being. Do you think that it's right that these guys get to live while my daughter is laying six feet underground?"

Mike took a deep breath, "Between you and me? Of course, it's not right. Everybody knows that. But there are laws…"

"I'm not asking you about laws!" Daylee cut him off, "I'm asking you if it's right or not! That's what I'm asking!"

"I know what you want me to say, and I'm not gonna say it."

"Why not? Has the police got you so programmed that you can't even give a simple yes or no answer?"

Now Mike stood up and yelled back at his childhood friend, "That's not fair, Daylee! That's not fucking fair!"

"What's not fair is those three ass wipes are still alive while my daughter is dead! That is what's not fair!"

After a moment, Daylee motioned to Mike to sit next to him, "I'm sorry, Mike. That was over the line. I didn't mean it."

"It's okay," Mike said, "I know what you want to do. I feel the same way. Nicole was like my own daughter too."

"Then help me find a way," Daylee said, "Help me find a way to make it fair. Help me find a way to kill these guys."

Mike got up and walked away.

Not more than five feet away from where Daylee and Mike were sitting was a funeral director who happened to overhear the entire conversation. He had just come back to the hearse parked near where the two men were sitting.

"Forgive me, sir. I'm not normally maha'oe, but I happened to hear your conversation."

Daylee tried to brush the man off, "You didn't hear anything. Just go away."

Insistent, the funeral director went on, "If what I heard was correct, then I know a way to help you make things fair. Come back to this same spot in three days at twelve, noon, and I will be here."

Daylee looked the funeral director over for a minute. He was a tall, thin man in a plain, blue suit and tie. There was nothing remarkable about the Hawaiian man except for his stark, white hair and piercing, black eyes. Daylee noticed how large and calloused his hands were. There was also a kind of energy to him that Daylee couldn't figure out. It was the kind of energy that put itself out but also took back.

"You don't have to say anything just now," the funeral director remarked, "Three days. You'll find me here, in this same spot, in three days."

"Really?" Daylee replied, "And exactly how are you going to help me?"

"Ah," the funeral director laughed, "There are much too much people here in this cemetery today. They may hear us. Better that you return in three days and I will tell you everything you need to know. I must hurry now. I have another appointment."

With that, the funeral director got into his hearse and drove off toward the main building. Daylee returned to Nicole's services.

44

Later that night, Daylee had an unusual dream that he was back at the cemetery, and it was daylight. Nicole was sitting on the same concrete bench where he and Mike sat earlier that day.

"Dad, don't," Nicole said in the dream. Her mouth wasn't moving, but he could hear her voice in his head, "Don't, Dad."

Just then, the hearse that the funeral director drove appeared behind Nicole on the small lane. Nicole looked back at the car and looked at Daylee again, and said, "Dad, don't."

Daylee was taking some sliced salami out of the refrigerator when he overheard the interview on the news the next morning. Leena was riveted to the television screen by the time he got to the living room. The young female news reporter was wearing a serious demeanor as she asked the two young men a series of questions.

The woman was standing in front of a house in Salt Lake on Likini Street. She had been granted an exclusive interview with Gary Catao and Jermel Evans.

"Describe what happened that evening when you saw Nicole Kaho'ohuli in the parking structure at Cooke Field?"

"Woll," Gary Catao said, "She had a bunch of books in her arms when she was getting out of her car…"

"Yeah," Jermel continued, "So we saw that she was struggling and offered our help, and I guess we surprised her because that's when she dropped her books and started attacking us."

"That's a fucking lie!" Daylee screamed, "She was going to a dance class that night! She didn't have any fucking books with her! She only had her dance bag! Fucking liars!"

On Wednesday at precisely twelve noon, Daylee drove up to the bench near the statue of Christ in the Mililani Cemetery. Waiting just off to the side of the bench was the funeral director. As Daylee drove up closer, he also noticed Mike leaning up against the left end of the statue.

Getting out of his car now, he approached the two men, "Oh, I see! This whole thing was a scam, so you're here to arrest this guy!"

The funeral director looked over at Mike and smiled, "He's your friend. Would you like to tell him, or should I?"

"Tell me what? What's going on? You know this guy?"

Looking over at the funeral director Mike said, "I'll do it."

"And to think," The funeral director continued, "You were going to walk away from your childhood friend even after he asked."

"The best thing I could have done for him was walk away," Mike shot back.

The funeral director looked at Mike seriously and said, "Tell him. Or I will."

With that, the funeral director walked down the lane toward the main building.

'What the hell was that all about?" Daylee asked.

Mike's whole demeanor suddenly changed. It wasn't the work face. It was the face of someone Daylee didn't know. Daylee had never seen him this way before.

"I'm sorry, Daylee. I really am."

"For what?"

"For this," Mike quickly stood up and threw a blinding right hook to Daylee's jaw and knocked him out cold.

When Daylee awoke, he found himself in the middle of a massive-sized heiau that overlooked the west and east end of ʻOʻahu. His head was still spinning, and the left side of his jaw felt tight, but it wasn't swollen. The area was illuminated by the bright stars and an even brighter full moon. If not for those two elements, the entire structure would have been pitch-black. He could make out a figure standing just outside the east end of the heiau. When his eyes became a bit more acclimated to the dark, he could see that it was Mike.

"You okay?"

47

"My jaw is kinda stiff, but I'm okay," now losing his temper, Daylee screamed, "What the fuck Mike?"

"You wanted fair? I'm giving you fair."

"This is fair?" Daylee yelled, "Asshole!"

Daylee noticed that the heiau was located in the middle of a vast open area. What was strange is that even though he could hear Mike from outside the temple, whenever he spoke, the sound of his voice would just drop off right in front of him.

"What is this, Mike? What's going on?"

"This heiau is built on a vortex. You're standing in the middle of it. It's active. It's working right now. Look at your hands."

Looking at his palms, he saw that they were black with what looked like soot, "Why are my hands painted black, Michael?"

"That's not paint," Mike replied, "Those are the ashes."

"Ashes of what?" Daylee shrieked.

"In a short time, you won't be able to hear my voice anymore. Sit down right where you are and think about Nicole. Think about everything that happened to her and think about the men who were involved in her killing. Don't think of anything else but that. Sit down, right now, Daylee, and think."

Soon Daylee could only see Mike's mouth moving, but he couldn't hear him anymore. Daylee sat right on the spot he was just standing, and it didn't take him long to think about what happened to Nicole. It wasn't too long also before his heart was filled with a black rage, and he could envision himself piercing a knife through the heart of each man. He began to think about Nicole fighting for her life and being killed so brutally by this Fowler McGuire. His temples began to pound, and his heart was racing now. His fists clenched, and his jaw tightened even more. No wedding. No grandchildren. No more family holidays.

"No," he thought, "No."

It began to build inside him. He could feel it swelling up from his gut. It was surging now like a storm.

"NOOOOOOO!" came the primal scream, "NOOOOOOOOOOOOO! I'LL KILL YOU! I'LL KILL YOU! WHY DID YOU KILL MY DAUGHTER? WHY!"

Daylee screamed again and again and again until his voice went hoarse, and he was spent. As he sat there with his body shaking in tears, he suddenly heard a deep gravelly voice from behind him that shook the very ground that he sat on.

"Eia au."

Daylee whirled around on his behind to see a massive, shadowy figure that was beginning to take shape right in front of him. He looked toward the heiau's east wall and saw that Mike was now on his hands and knees with his head down.

As the figure approached, Daylee asked, "'O wai la 'oe? Who are you?"

"'O au 'o Lua. I am Lua," came the reply, "Ho'ike mai ia'u kou lima."

Daylee held his palms open facing the figure, and the figure grabbed both Daylee's hands between his own. Daylee felt his hands burning, but the shock and pain were so tremendous, he was unable to scream.

"'Ike pono au ka inaina i loko ou. 'O ia ke kumu aia au 'ia ne'i. I thoroughly see the rage within you. This is the reason I am here."

Then the figure lets Daylee go. He crumbles to the ground and soon realizes that the pain is gone. He looks at his hands, but there are no sores or scars. His hands are perfectly fine save for the palms, which are blackened from ashes of unknown origin.

The figure looks over at Mike and says, "Ku a'e."

Mike stood up. He adeptly stepped over the wall of the heiau and, as he approached the figure, he bowed his head as if he were approaching someone sacred. He knelt next to Daylee and put his arms around him.

Under his breath, Daylee tells Mike, "I have to ask him something."

Mike is completely floored, "No. You've already asked. Once is enough. No one ever asks twice."

Before Mike could stop him, Daylee opens his mouth, "Pehea ka uku?"

"Ke ola," the figure replies with the slightest grin.

Mike immediately prostrates to the ground and forces Daylee's head down to the dirt beside him, "Idiot."

Darkness then enveloped the figure.

"What's the big rush?" Daylee asks as Mike is hurriedly forcing him out of the heiau.

"The Mahealani Moon is hiding behind the clouds now. Once she appears, this entire heiau will disappear. If we're not out of here in time, once it's gone, so are we!"

They cross the east wall of the heiau just as the light of the moon touches the earth and the entire heiau seemed to dissolve, leaving nothing but an empty field of pili grass.

Daylee is exhausted and tells Mike that he can explain everything later, "Right now, I'm going to kick your ass!"

All Mike says is, "About that..." and knocks Daylee out again with a wicked right cross.

At ten–thirty on Thursday morning, Daylee wakes up on the couch in his own living room. Leena is applying a cold compress to his forehead and is clearly upset.

"You know, I can understand you're upset because of Nicole's passing, but that doesn't mean you have to drag Mike out with you all night to go drinking at some goddamned bar with naked women dancing on the stage! And poor thing, look at Mike! He fell asleep over there on the armchair, all stinking drunk! What the hell is wrong with you? Don't you know Mike had to work today? Now he's gonna get in trouble cause of you!" Pressing the compress harder into his forehead, she yells at him once more, "Hold this damn thing yourself, I gotta go work!"

Daylee is speechless and confused as Leena walks out the door, gets into her car, and drives off.

Mike bolts upright from his chair and says, "She left already?"

Daylee moans, "Oh, my head is pounding. Mike, try come get this thing off my head. Leena put too much ice. It's burning my skin."

"Sure," Mike walks over to where Daylee is lying on the couch.

As soon as Mike gets near enough, Daylee punches him in the groin. Mike drops to his knees in agony. Even with his head pounding, Daylee manages to run into the kitchen, grabs Leena's heaviest frying pan, and folds the entire pan over Mike's head. Daylee is furious.

"What, brah? You like try false crack me two times?"

Mike is trying his best to crawl away as Daylee goes back into the kitchen in search of Leena's heavy cookie sheet.

Daylee screams, "How's dis for one false crack?" and hits Mike square between the shoulder blades.

As he readies himself for a second swing, he is suddenly pushed forcefully across the living room. He lands on the couch and flips over backward. He gets up on his knees and looks over the couch, and sees Mike on the other side of the room in an open palm thrust stance, his palms jet black with the same ashes Daylee's palms were stained with earlier. Just as it dawns on Daylee what happened, the blackness on Mike's palms fades away.

"Sit down," Mike says, "So I can explain everything."

Daylee says, "Explain from ova dea. You not going false crack me again, brah!"

"Alright, just sit down then."

"No, fuck you! Why you had to false crack me, brah?"

"You still stuck on that? You stupid or what? The funeral director called me last minute 'cause you're my friend. We're supposed to use chloroform to knock you out but never have, so I had to improvise."

"I changed my mind. Why you no come over here so I can improvise my foot up your ass?"

"Look," Mike said, "I'm sorry. But once I explain everything to you, you'll understand, and you won't be so mad."

"Okay," said Daylee, "But first thing, you better tell me why my wife thinks we went strip club last night and got all drunk!"

"Alright, alright," Mike tells him, "Just sit down. Just listen."

"Okay, I'll listen, but I ain't sitting down. I don't trust you no more."

8:00am the same morning on Likini Street at Radford Terrace, Catao residence.

The loud banging on Gary Catao's bedroom door continued for nearly 40 minutes before he finally woke up. It had only been less than a month, but he was still dizzy from the beating he suffered at Nicole's hands. The pounding on the door didn't make him feel any better.

"Why the hell is she home? She should be at work right now making her customers' lives miserable, not mine!" Gary muttered to himself before he began shouting at his mother, "What the hell is it? Whattaya want ma, for chrissakes?"

"Get up and go take a shower and find a job! NOW! You and your friends' real tough guys, hah? You go try rape one girl, and when she turn around kick your guys' ass, you cannot handle, so you have to go run her ovah wit one car? Den you go on the news and lie dat you folks was trying for help her after dey wen already show the tape from the security camera? What a dumbass! No wonder why your boss went fire you! I dunno how I went get one son like you!"

Infuriated, Gary opened his bedroom door and was ready to be in his mother's face in no time flat. Except that it wasn't his mother standing outside his bedroom door. It was a tall shadowy figure with the outline of what looked like a human being but without the details. In a fraction of a second, the figure thrust its right hand into the space just below Gary's sternum and tore out his liver. Even before the pain could register in Gary's brain, the figure then scooped Gary's eyes out with the fingers on its left hand. It then held Gary's eyes and liver up above its head as if it were making some kind of offering. By the time Gary's lifeless body fell to the floor, the figure had already eaten what it had so effortlessly taken from its victim.

Esmerelda Catao would return home to find the body of her son lying in an almost black pool of blood just outside his bedroom door. Because the neighbors had become accustomed to Esmerelda screaming at her son at all hours, it would be a while before they finally came to check on her and see what was happening. It was an interesting experience because they would end up screaming just as loud once they saw what Esmerelda had found.

Two hours later, at Hobron Square in Waikiki, Jermel Evans stood in the dance studio next to Keola, the hula instructor for the Hula Lima Lu'au Show. Facing the mirror in front of them, Jermel did his best to follow Keola as they went over the first verse of a hula kahiko called "Kawika."

"E ia no Kawika e i e, ka heke a'o na pua e i e. Right kaholo, left kaholo, hands and arms out to both sides and pua motion to the front middle."

"I'm not feeling it," Jermel said.

"I know," Keola replied, "It's been twenty-five minutes, and we're still stuck on the first verse. Listen, maybe you should tell yourself that you're not cut out for this. I need dancers that get it in the first five minutes."

"Are you a Kumu Hula?" Jermel asked.

"No, but I'm the dance and line captain for the lu'au show," Keola smirked.

Jermel walked out of the studio and went back to his car. His girlfriend, Sherayne, who sat in the car the whole time, waiting, asked Jermel right away, "So? Did you get it? It was easy, right? Kawika? That dance is a hula standard, so it should have been duck soup, right?"

"Nah. The guy isn't even a real Kumu Hula. I cannot dance for somebody like that," Jermel said, "I just left."

"Jermel," Sherayne was mildly irritated, "Did you get it or not?"

"I just told you I left!" Jermel yelled.

Very calmly, Sherayne replied, "Today and only today that Lu'au Show is paying people fifty dollars cash if they get the job, TODAY. Fifty dollars will give us enough to put forty dollars in the car for gas, and then we'd have ten dollars left over to eat lunch at McDonald's. You go back in there right now, and you kiss ass to that guy even if he's not a kumu hula, and you get that job. Otherwise, I'm dropping your worthless ass today, Jermel. Do you understand? After what happened with that girl, you still think that you have the right to act like a prick to me?"

"I didn't do anything to that girl. That was all Fowler," Jermel said smugly.

"Of course, you didn't do anything, Jermel," Sherayne said sweetly, "You never got the chance because that girl kicked all of your asses. It's all over YouTube and the news. She kicked you square in the nuts and left you lying on the ground while she beat the shit out of Gary. And if Fowler hadn't run away like the little bitch that he is, she would have fucked his shit up too. However, out of the three, YOU were the most pathetic. Lying on the grown all curled up and helpless. Some tough guy you are, huh? Go back in there and make that paper bitch."

Jermel's looked changed as if he was going to hit Sherayne, but instead, he got out of the car and headed back to the dance studio. Heading back up the stairs now, he noticed that one of the light bulbs on the landing must have gone out because it was dark in most of the left corner. However, when he reached the top of the stairs, he saw that the light bulb was working just fine. He couldn't figure out what was it that was casting the shadow in the corner. It almost seemed to be there of its own free will. Jermel stepped closer to it and saw that it looked like a simple shadow from something he couldn't see. He had intended to mention it to Keola when he saw him, but he would never get the chance.

The figure appeared without warning and grabbed Jermel by the ankles, lifted him off the floor, and threw him back down on his head. Jermel was too dazed to react. With two hands wrapped around Jermel's right ankle and its left foot stepping on the middle of Jermel's thigh, the figure placed its right foot next to Jermel's head and, with one short, fast pull, it tore Jermel's body into two pieces. Working quickly, the figure knelt down next to the body and removed the liver, and held it up over its head, offering a prayer of supplication before it consumed what it had taken.

That very same day in Kalihi, back at the Kahoʻohuli residence, Mike's explanation of the previous night's events and the story of the Black Hand Society didn't sit well with Daylee. Even though it made sense and answered many questions, there still seemed to be something missing from the equation. Daylee had asked Mike to leave after that. He needed some time to think.

At noon, he was sitting at his kitchen table with his laptop in front of him. On the screen was the YouTube website with the feature of the week, which read, "LOSERS GET THEIR ASSES KICKED BY GIRL THEN KILL HER."

He wasn't sure why he was about to look at the video which recorded his daughter's brutal death, but there was an inner voice that told him that therein would be the answer that would satisfy the question in his heart. After a few more minutes, Daylee finally clicked on the PLAY icon, and the video began.

Nicole's Audi Quattro backed into the parking space at the Cooke field parking structure. The second her door opened, Gary, Jermel, and Fowler were on her. Daylee realized this as he replayed that part at :36 seconds, five times. This told Daylee that they were not only waiting for her but that they had been watching her every move for some time before finally mounting their attack. Fowler and Gary grab her by the shoulders first. Jermel reaches forward in what looks like an attempt to rip open Nicole's top, but Nicole lands a brutal kick to Jermel's groin and lifts him right off the ground. Everything is happening so fast now that Gary and Fowler haven't even realized what just happened to Jermel. Nicole reaches down behind her to her left and grabs Fowlers left ankle, and pulls up and front. Fowler takes a nasty spill on the back of his head. On the video, Daylee could hear the sickening sound of Fowler's head hitting the concrete pavement. In the same instant, Nicole spins around counter–clockwise to her left and delivers a punishing elbow to the side of Gary's skull. The impact of Nicole's elbow strike knocks Gary up against the door of her car. In the background, Daylee sees Fowler slowly crawling away and then getting to his feet. He stumbles twice and then disappears off of the left side of the screen.

After that, it's nearly another minute of footage where Nicole punishes Gary with a series of elbow strikes. Gary throws blind punches for a few seconds, but the elbow strikes are too fast and precise. Gary's legs start to give out from under him, but Nicole continually holds him up against her car, almost as if she is refusing to let him faint from the pain. Soon, Daylee sees that this has become a game to Nicole. When Gary covers up with his arms over his head, Nicole delivers short, burning jabs to his ribs. She's enjoying it. A chill comes over Daylee's body as he suddenly realizes that he is seeing a side of his daughter that he never knew existed. Something about the last few overhead elbow strikes catches Daylee's eye. Nicole brings her right elbow straight down on the top of Gary's head and knocks him senseless. It's a traditional elbow strike with the palm open. At first, it looks like a distortion or a glitch. Daylee plays it back and pauses the video at exactly 2:14. What he sees nearly takes the breath out of his body.

"Oh, my god," Daylee put his head down in disbelief, "Oh, my god."

Digging into his pocket, he finds his phone and calls Mike right away.

"Officer Nakamura."

.

"Mike, it's Daylee. Come get me now. We have to find Fowler McGuire. There's a killer out there, and if we don't get to this kid first, he's gonna die!"

The ghost of Nicole Kahoʻohuli stood in front of the Mercedes as it sat in the garage of the McGuire home in Manoa. Fowler had just started up the German sports car when the specter of the girl he murdered suddenly materialized out of nowhere. He now sat riveted to the steering wheel, too overcome with fear to even try and run. All Fowler could do was cry hysterically as he babbled incoherently about being sorry and begging for forgiveness.

Nicole's apparition dissipated for a second and reappeared as a black, undulating shadow that now let itself seep in through the car's air vents until it filled the Mercedes entirely. Fowler felt the oxygen leave the vehicle, and he began to choke for air. The shadow filled his lungs, and Fowler literally started to drown. His last conscious memory was the sound of something pounding the car window and screaming out a name. After that, everything went black.

At this point, the shadow had left Fowler's body and ripped the car door off its hinges. Dragging the young man's limp body out of the Mercedes, the shadow held him over its head and began to take on the outline of a human form.

"Leena! Leena, no! Put him down, Leena! Put him down!"

Mike and Daylee arrived at the McGuire home just in time. The figure recognized Daylee's voice and slowly turned to look at him.

"Leena! Put him down. Put him down, Leena. Let him go."

The figure dropped Fowler on the garage floor with a thud. The darkness that enveloped it slowly pulled away. All that was left was Leena Kahoʻohuli, standing there in the same clothes that she wore when she left the house earlier.

"Leena," Daylee pleaded, "Come here, honey. C'mon. Let's go home."

"Hun," Leena cried, "He killed our baby. He took our Nicole from us. Are we just supposed to let him and his friends go?"

"It's done Leena, it's over," Daylee said with finality.

"How did you know I'd be here?" Leena asked.

"The YouTube video, the one with Nicole," Daylee said.

"Oh, you shouldn't watch that video, Daylee!"

"Leena, at the end, when Nicole was hitting Gary Catao with overhand elbow strikes, her hand was open. Her palm was black."

"Let's go home, okay, honey?" Daylee held on to his wife with everything he had. After today, no one was ever going to know their secret.

That night, as Daylee lay in bed with his wife, he remembered their earlier conversation.

"How did you know to find me at that boy's house?"

"I told you, I watched the video. Nicole's hand was black. The natural conclusion is that she inherited her martial arts gift from you, a member of the Black Palm Society. Someone taught her how to fight that way, and it wasn't Michael. So, it could only have been you. It took me a while. You masked your pain well, but I realized you just faced it in a different way."

Watching her sleep, he thought about what Mike had told him earlier that morning. He would have to make it a point to see Mike later tonight. For now, Daylee just wanted to be with his wife, protecting her, loving her, and helping her work through her heartache.

1989. Somewhere in the mountains of Palehua near Mauna Kapu.

Mike Nakamura, Jack Pagdilao, Manny Fernandez, and Billy Mitchell were all practitioners of Kenpo Karate. Over the years, they had individually become affected in one way or another by personal tragedies in their lives.

Mike Nakamura's thirteen-year-old niece was raped and killed by a stranger as she walked home from Waipahu Intermediate one day, after school. The man forced her into his car and took her out to an old junkyard, where he bashed the back of her head in before raping her.

Jack Pagdilao's brother was gunned down in front of Arakawa's one morning because he refused to give up his wallet to a couple of young punks. The two were never caught, even though there were seven eyewitnesses who saw it happen.

Billy Mitchell was assaulted by a large mob of local men because they believed that he was disrespecting them by crossing their basketball court late at night.

Manny Fernandez watched in horror as his sister's jealous ex-boyfriend ran her over with his Chevelle after seeing her kiss Manny goodbye on the cheek at a family party at the Visayan Club in Waipahu. Manny was the only one to come forward and testify as an eyewitness. The jealous ex-boyfriend got off due to a lack of evidence and credible witnesses aside from Manny.

The four martial arts instructors had finally had enough. They wanted to do something about the injustice that seemed to be prevalent in their society. Coincidentally, Jack, Mike, and Billy were classmates with Manny's sister at Campbell High School. After attending her funeral services at Mililani Cemetery, they gravitated towards one another. They found themselves sitting on the concrete bench next to the statue of Christ.

Manny was the first to express his disgust with the justice system and its vigorous efforts to support the criminal rather than the victim. He wanted something fair. He wanted his sister's ex-boyfriend to pay with his life. Jack, Billy, and Mike felt the same way. A life should be sacrificed for the life it took. Death should be the payment.

That's when they met the funeral director who had conveniently been listening as he had just helped a small group of pallbearers remove a casket from the back of his hearse. He didn't really introduce himself, but he did promise them that if they met him in the same exact spot where they were sitting now, three days hence when the sun was high overhead and cast no shadow, he would be able to help them resolve their problem.

In three days, the men were back in the same place where the funeral director was already waiting for them with a limousine.

"Please, I'll take you to where we need to go, and you will have all your answers."

Soon, they were on their way to their intended destination. The funeral director told the men that the drive would be rather long, so he encouraged them to help themselves to any drinks in the bar. There were only cans of Pepsi, which they each drank. It was the last thing they remembered. When they awoke, they were in the middle of a massive heiau at the top of a mountain where they could clearly see the east and west end of ʻOʻahu. Standing outside the west wall of the heiau was the funeral director.

"I'm sorry that things had to be done this way, but this location is secret. It's been in my family for as long as anyone one of us can remember. Each of you asked that the lives of those who killed your ʻohana be taken as payment for their deeds. I am going to help you fulfill that wish. This temple is dedicated to the god, Kuʻi a lua. This is where the martial art of bone breaking was practiced; this is where the art of sorcery was taught alongside it. You will learn lua in this temple. The training will be brutal and harsh, but should you complete this training, you will be unstoppable. You will move like a shadow, and there will be no trace of you when your work is done. No one will know who we are or where we meet, save for one person. My family line is dying out, and this knowledge must somehow survive. I now pass down everything I know to you. Help is coming. Prepare yourselves."

In an instant, the massive shadowy figure appeared and blackened the four men's hands with its own. From that night and every night forward, they would return to learn every aspect of lua from the funeral director who stood outside the west wall of the heiau and gave instruction to the men who were trained by the shadowy figure. The time would finally come when their training was complete. The four men were able to go out into society and mete out justice in their own, very unique way.

Twenty–three years later. Mauna Kapu.

"There was one big hole in that story Mike," Daylee said.

"What is that?" Mike asked.

"You forgot the fifth person. Leena, the funeral director's daughter. You left that part out. She was there training right alongside you guys the whole time. You tell me everything now, Mike. Tell me."

"I'll tell him," the voice came from behind. It was Leena.

"Hun," Leena began, "This is how we've been able to help people out whose family members are killed and cannot find justice. My father overhears certain conversations, and he decides which people need our services the most."

"When we first met, you said that your parents had died when you were a baby and that you never knew who they were," Daylee thought for a second, and then it made sense to him, "Okay, okay, now I understand."

"The day he overheard your conversation and called me, I immediately called Mike, and we had to decide quickly about what we were going to do. We never wanted this for you, hun. It's really not the kind of life to live, but this is who we are. You see, my father never attends any of the funeral services. He only hears the conversations afterward. He has never met you and had no idea who you were," Leena explained.

"But he knew Nicole. He must have trained her himself at some point?" Daylee asked.

"No," Leena replied, "Our daughter was a prodigy. She was coming into it on her own. She has never been to the heiau. She's never met the shadow. All my father and I and the rest of us could do was point her in the right direction. Those poor boys made a mistake in attacking her that night. She was going to kill them. But as for you, hun, we had to decide how we were going to do this. My father had already set everything in motion, and we had to follow through."

"So that whole thing about the bar and you being mad at me was an act?" Daylee asked.

"Yeah," Mike said, "Of course, the frying pan and the cookie sheet was all you."

"So what happens now?"

"You receive your training," Leena says, "This heiau is protected by Mauna Kapu and appears in the pitch black. The Mahealani moon phase protects it and puts it under her sacred kapa. It's a special place. Manny, Jack, and Billy will be here soon, and we'll all help you. Okay, honey?"

"Alright," Daylee agreed.

When the first phase of training was completed, and Daylee and Leena returned home, they both slept for most of the day. In Daylee's dream, he saw Nicole standing outside of the heiau's west wall at Mauna Kapu.

"This is why I said, 'Don't Dad.' I was afraid that you might get hurt or that you may not understand," she said.

"I understand now," Daylee replied.

"Then you understand that you don't have to be sad for me?"

"I'm sad that I lost you so soon," Daylee said.

"You taught me to never fear and to always fight until the last if I knew I was right. It's because of you, Dad, that I was never afraid. Even on the night I died, I had no fear. I knew I was right. I died fighting until the last, just like you taught me," Nicole said.

Through his tears, Daylee said, "Baby, I wish I could hold you one more time and tell you how much I love you."

"I know you love me, Dad. I could always feel it everywhere I went. I'll be with you whenever you go to Mauna Kapu."

In the dream, the Mahealani moon appeared, and Nicole slowly faded away along with the heiau.

Daylee asked for something that was born from the grief and rage of his own heart and received that which he wanted. And much more.

NOBUO

IN THE YEAR 2008, I was granted permission by the powers that be to take a small group of people on a ghost tour inside the 'Iolani Palace. It was summer, so I required that everyone who participated that evening wear the color white from head to toe in honor of Obon. It was exciting to see so many people dressed in white entering and leaving our only Royal Palace in the United States. It must have made quite an impression on those passersby who happened to witness such an unusual event. After the short tour of the Palace, a charter bus took us to the Japanese Cemetery in Mo'ili'ili. There, I would bring the group to visit Miles Fukunaga's grave and share other haunted stories associated with the area.

When we arrived, the group walked ahead of me, following my assistant. As I walked down the paved lane, I happened to see a petite Japanese boy sitting on the curb in front of a small, white marble headstone with Japanese characters written on it. I hadn't noticed him earlier at the Palace because I was much too concerned with making sure that no one touched broke anything while we were inside.

Sitting there with his knees folded up to his chest and his arms wrapped around his legs, he looked to be a bit out of place in his coat and hat. However, I had to consider that this was Obon season, so perhaps there was a reason why his parents chose to dress him this way. I was a bit upset because here was a boy who looked to be no more than six or seven years old sitting on the ground by himself, and his parents didn't even notice that he was gone from their side.

Gesturing down the lane toward Miles' headstone, I asked the boy, "Are your parents over there?"

Looking toward where I was pointing, the boy shook his head and replied, "No. I'm only waiting for my Mommy."

Now I was even more irritated. Who leaves their kid in a cemetery late at night to wait? Bad parenting.

"Is your mommy over there with the rest of that group?"

"No," he shook his head again, "She told me she was coming to bring me guava juice and Bazooka bubble gum."

In my head, I reminded myself to give this little boy's mother a piece of my mind when she did show up to bring him his snack. Extending my hand to the boy now, I told him, "Why don't you come with me until your mommy shows up? It's safer that way. We'll go right over there with all the other people."

Looking toward Miles' headstone again, the little boy said, "I wanted to talk to you about that. Every time you come here, you always go talk to that guy. You never say hello to me, and you never say goodbye. You always just come and go. That guy always gets visits. Me, I just have to wait until my mommy comes."

A chill came over my entire body as I realized what was going on and what this boy was.

"I'll make sure that I say hello and goodbye from now on," I promised him, "But tell me about how you got here?"

"I don't know," he began, "I was sick. My mommy was by my bed, and she was washing my body with a wet cloth. She kept telling me it would be alright, and she promised to bring me my favorite stuffs, guava juice, and Bazooka Bubble Gum. Mommy was crying. So, I have to wait here for my Mommy to come."

Choking back my tears, I promised the boy that I would always say hello and goodbye from now on. I then said that I had to join the group of people waiting for me.

"Can I come with you?" he asked. He now seemed terribly lonely.

My reply to him nearly broke my heart, but there was nothing I could do.

"No," I said, "What if your mom comes and you're not here? She'll be worried. You don't want to make her worry, right?"

He seemed to be resigned to that fact, and, for a moment, his eyes were looking down as if he were trying to make sense of it all.

"Oh yeah," he whispered to himself, "I better wait then."

I turned away from him to join my group and finish out the last part of the tour. As we were leaving, we passed the boy's headstone, but he was no longer there.

"Bye," I said softly, "I'll be back."

The following evening, I returned to the Japanese Cemetery with a smaller group. I shared my experience from the night before.

A woman from Japan who was on the tour blurted out in perfect English, "He's right. There is definitely a little Japanese boy here. Those Japanese characters on the headstone say his name is Nobuo. It's the boy's name for the afterlife, not his name while he lived."

As it turned out, this woman claimed she is a psychic. She had been very unassuming the entire evening. Hence, her reaction to the experience I just shared with the rest of the group came as a surprise. What she went on to say also proved to be a validation of what had transpired the night before.

"The boy's last memory was that he was sick, but he was actually dying in a hospital here in Honolulu. His mother washed his body so that he would be clean before going into the next world. She was grief–stricken and kept saying that it would be okay and that she

would bring him his favorite things that he loved, Bazooka Bubble Gum and guava juice. What she meant was that she would bring those things with her into the afterlife when she had passed. The little boy didn't know. All he knew was that, at the very last moment of his life, the last thing he heard was the voice of his mother promising to bring him his favorite thing in the whole wide world. That promise has kept him here sitting in front of his headstone waiting for her."

I put my head down and fought back the tears. Had I lost my own child, I would have been filled with as much grief as the mother of this boy must have been. Her world must have fallen apart at that moment. A cool wind appeared suddenly, and it seemed to have embraced each one of us as we stood there in front of this child's grave. It seemed pointless then to continue on and talk about Miles Fukunaga. I would save that for another time.

What are the last words you would like for your loved ones to hear before they part from this earthly plane? What are the last words you would like to hear before leaving the house or before someone you love leaves your side? Think carefully. The last words a person hears may give someone the freedom to move on or cause one to remain right where he or she is.

NAʻU
Mine

AFTER LIVING A FULL LIFE, Emma Kaneuila, was now near the end of her time on our earthly plane. At the age of 86, it had been a few months since her last routine checkup, but she began to feel out of sorts. Suddenly, she could no longer do the things she liked to do or move in the way she used to. So it was Mae's suggestion that she go for a checkup just to see.

On the day of her appointment, Emma noticed that she was bleeding. It had been years since she had had her maʻi, so she thought that the occurrence was quite unusual. It began as a simple spot of blood that did not bother her severely. She changed clothes, and soon she was on her way to the doctor's office as scheduled. However, she had not even driven a few blocks from her home when she began to bleed more heavily. She immediately returned home to find that her niece, Kaʻiulani, had not yet left for work. Emma called the young girl to her car and asked her to bring out some wet towels to wipe down her car seat. While the young girl performed this duty, Emma went into the house to call 911.

After cleaning her Aunty's car, Ka'iulani went into the house and found Emma almost slumped over while sitting at the kitchen table. The girl quickly took Emma into her arms to keep her from falling off her chair and hitting the floor.

"Mama Emma! Are you okay? What happened? Why is all that blood on your car seat?" Ka'iulani cried.

"I think," Emma said, "I may be terribly sick. I called for an ambulance, and they should be here shortly. Do not say anything about this until the doctor tells me what's wrong. Do you understand?"

The girl nodded in agreement.

"In case it turns out to be nothing, I don't want to send the family into a panic unnecessarily."

In a short time, the ambulance arrived, and Emma was brought to the Straub Hospital emergency room. Emma's doctor came down from his office to see her. He ordered several tests, including an ultrasound, then an MRI. When he returned, he simply told Emma that he wasn't quite sure what the problem may be and that he would have to perform a few more tests to be sure. Emma wasn't buying it.

"Dr. Reyes," Emma began, "I'm an old woman, but I'm not a stupid one. I've lived a long time and, over these years, I've come to develop an internal bullshit meter.

Right now, my meter is ticking, and it's telling me that you are full of it."

Looking her in the eye, Dr. Reyes asked, "Are there any family members waiting for you in the lobby?"

"Yes," Emma said, "My niece Ka'iulani."

"I'll go get her. I'll be right back."

A short time later, as Ka'iulani sat at her Aunty's bedside. They watched Dr. Reyes standing there uncomfortably as if he were fighting to get the words out. Finally, as he spoke, his eyes began to tear over.

"Mrs. Kaneuila... you've been coming to me for many, many years, and I've come to know you as if you were my own mother, so..."

Emma reached out and held the doctor's hand softly in her own.

"It's alright, Dr. Reyes, just tell me straight. It's not as if we're breaking up, and we'll never see each other again, right?" Emma smiled.

"I wish it were that simple. Emma... I believe you may have pancreatic cancer. It's in a very late stage. Had we been able to diagnose it earlier, we might have been able to catch it, and..." Dr. Reyes couldn't finish.

Ka'iulani began to cry until her Aunty stopped her, "You have no time to cry, Ka'iulani. There is work to do."

Looking back at Dr. Reyes, she said, "Doctor, I am fully aware that there is no cure for pancreatic cancer. Earlier or later, the result would be the same. Kaʻiulani, I need you to prepare lunch for tomorrow at home. We are going to have company, so you have to make enough to feed the whole family, do you understand?"

Kaʻiulani quickly composed herself, took out a notepad from her purse, and began to prepare a menu for the following day.

"Mrs. Kaneuila, there's treatment for your condition even this late in the game. I'll make every effort to extend your life as long as possible," Dr. Reyes said.

Emma laughed, "Ha! There you go again, bullshitting me! I know what you're trying to do, Daryl, and I aloha you for that but all that chemotherapy and tests and needles? You may as well pull the plug now. No, I'm too old, and my body won't survive that. I'll go with what dignity I have left, and I'll die at home."

On the drive home, Emma instructed her niece to call her Aunty Mae, Emma's older sister, and have her come to her house that evening. When Mae arrived with her husband, Luther, she sat them down and broke the news to the two of them. They were just as devastated as Kaʻiulani was earlier in the day, and they received the same reprimand as the girl did.

"There is no time for tears, Mae. I need you to call everyone tonight and tell them to be here for lunch. Say that it's an important announcement."

"You know how your daughter is, Emma. Unless it's about her, she won't come," Mae said.

"Then tell her that it's about money. She'll be here with her whole brood in tow," Emma replied sharply.

Mae made all of the phone calls to the family while Ka'iulani prepared lunch for everyone. The following day, when the gathering was underway and everyone was well fed for the afternoon, Ka'iulani had them assemble in the living room where Emma was sitting in her favorite koa rocking chair.

"Aloha mai kakou, my precious 'ohana. Mahalo to everyone for coming here on such short notice," looking over at her older sister, Mae, Emma said, "Thank you, Mae, for calling everyone."

Her older sister smiled and put her hand to her lips.

Looking now at her niece, she said, "And you, my precious Ka'iulani. Thank you for feeding everyone."

Taking a deep breath, Emma began, "Yesterday, I found out from my doctor that I have pancreatic cancer and that it has already spread too far. As a result of that, I am beyond any treatment, save for the doctors giving me a shot from which I would never wake up."

82

She gave her family a moment to let the news sink in. Many of her family were immediately grief-stricken and wept without restraint. Mae held on to her younger sister's hand as Emma regained her composure and spoke again.

"Because my husband Henry has long since passed, half of my money will go to my son, Thayer, and his family. Thayer, you've grown into a fine man and a great husband and father. Your papa would be very proud of you were he alive today. Thank you for being a good son."

Thayer held on to his mother's hands and cried. Realizing the truth of what his mother was saying broke his heart. She would never be there to share in his children's first prom, graduation, or wedding. It was hard for him to take. He was finally led away by his wife, who lent him comfort as they stood in the corner of their mother's living room.

"Dianne," Emma looked at her firstborn, "Your money will come to you only after you have proven that you can hold a regular job for a year. An attorney will see to the details of this. He will get copies of your pay stubs and the statements from your checking account. He will make sure that you save some of that money to feed your family and pay your rent and other bills in a timely manner. After that, you'll get your inheritance and not before."

Sitting on an oversized couch directly across from her mother with her newest infant child in her arms and her four other children hovering about her, Dianne was not pleased.

"Is this why you called me here? So that you could make me shame in front of everybody else?"

"No," Emma said.

"Well, why then? Why the hell would you do something like this? Thayer gets his damned money no problem! Why am I made to suffer?"

"I did this so that you and your husband wouldn't use the money I give you to buy pakalolo instead of taking care of your family."

"You go to hell, Mom! You go straight to hell!" Dianne was furious and couldn't hold her tongue. The room went silent for a second, then, without warning, Luther flew across the room, intending to slap his niece for her open disrespect of her mother.

Emma cried out, "No, Luther! Let her go, just let her go."

Withdrawing to his wife's side, Luther stared at Dianne with a boiling fury.

"Your mother ova hea dying, and you talk to her like that? You try one more time to talk to your mother like dat and I give you one wallop! Maopopo ia 'oe?"

Dianne knew he meant business and could only utter a weak, "Yes, Uncle Luther."

Dianne's husband had become so emasculated by her over the years that he never quite knew when to step in or when to keep his mouth shut. His timing was always wrong, and he could never do the right thing in her eyes.

Glaring at her husband, Richard, she growled, "Thanks for defending me, Mr. Weak Ass." Richard could only respond with his cultivated look of helplessness. Emma continued with what she had to say.

"Mae, this house will go to you and Luther."

Mae could only protest her sister's decision, "Emma, you don't need to leave the house to me. Luther and I already have our own home."

"You two live in an apartment on Kinau Street, Mae. You take the house. It's only right that you should live in the place where you grew up. I'll hear no more about it. The matter is settled."

Mae turned and smiled at Luther, who could only nod in agreement with his sister-in-law's declaration.

Turning now to her niece, Emma continued, "Ka'iulani, my dear one. Come. Mai."

With her arms outstretched, Emma reached for her niece, who softly embraced her aunt.

"Ka'iulani. You came to me as an infant child after your father and mother died so suddenly in that car accident. I raised you as my own, along with your two cousins. To you, I pass down all of our family history. Our godly and chiefly lineage, our spirituality, and our hardship as a people who are treated like house guests in our own land. You have always done all that I have asked without complaining even once. This is why I leave you my lei niho palaoa. It is a true mark of distinction as an Ali'i family who can rightfully claim their heritage.

"Our name, Kaneuila, is for the god of lightning. There is an old tale in our genealogy that the god Kaneuila took human form and came down from the heavens for a short time and lived among the common people. In his guise as a human being, he also became a victim to being flesh and blood.

"He met a human woman and fell deeply in love with her. They married and had a child who grew up to become a great Ali'i. His name was Kaneuila, like his godly father. At the appropriate time, he was married to a pi'o chiefess from Maui. From their children came the many generations of family that would eventually trickle down to myself and then to you. You will find the box in my bedroom closet on the top shelf. Bring it to me so that I can place it around your neck."

Kaʻiulani held on to her aunt and cried even more, "Mama Emma, I would rather that you live many more years here with me instead of having the lei niho palaoa! You keep it, Mama Emma, and you live. That's all I care about."

Richard whispered to his wife, "Isn't that supposed to go to you first, being the oldest daughter?"

Dianne laughed out loud and now addressed her mother directly, "Geez, Mom, you're still holding to that old legend? I've told you so many times to take that whale tooth pendant to the Bishop Museum and trade it in for money. It hasn't done anything for our "Aliʻi" status at all. What a joke!"

"Can you just shut up and show some damned respect?" Thayer yelled, "Mom is dying, and all you can think about is yourself!"

"Shut up, momma's boy," Dianne countered.

"Shut it, now!" Luther interrupted.

While the heated feelings began to permeate the room, Kaʻiulani was already looking through her aunt's closet. The rectangular-shaped box seemed to be a bit light considering what the contents were. Bringing the box to Emma, Kaʻiulani placed it gently on her Aunty's lap. As Emma removed the box's cover and pulled back the wax paper, she saw nothing but emptiness. There was no reaction on her face. If she was upset, sad, or infuriated, she wasn't showing it.

"Oh, my god, it's gone!" Mae gasped.

The entire family gathered around Emma and couldn't believe their eyes. Dianne gloated and couldn't hold her tongue as usual.

"I told you."

"Luther," Mae commanded, "Call the police and report a theft!"

Sitting quietly on her rocking chair, Emma said, "It's alright. There isn't any need for that. Whoever took it is a member of this household, but they are not true family."

Ka'iulani was confused, "How can that be Mama? It couldn't have been any one of us. We've all been here in the living room the whole time."

"There is no need for anyone to try and figure out who took it, so please, everyone, be calm and don't get upset," Emma replied.

"How can we not be upset?" Thayer asked, "That's a family heirloom!"

Putting her hands up as a kind of symbol to calm everyone down, Emma said, "Whoever took my lei niho palaoa will be at my ho'olewa. All of you here will know who that person is because you will witness it yourselves."

"Mom," Dianne said, "Now you're talking all that heebee-jeebee stuff. How are we supposed to know who took your whale tooth pendant at your funeral?"

"Because," Emma continued, "I will look that person in the eye from my casket, and by that, the thief will be marked by the gods of our family."

"It wasn't me!" Richard exclaimed, "I didn't take it, so don't look at me from your casket for God's sake, please, Emma!"

Ignoring her son-in-law, Emma took Ka'iulani's hands in hers and said, "At that moment, Ka'iulani, when the thief is revealed, that person will fall dead at your feet."

With no further explanation, Emma stood up from her rocking chair and retired to her bedroom to rest.

Two weeks later, as Ka'iulani readied herself for work, she stopped in briefly to check up on her Aunty Emma. The old woman was fast asleep, but she appeared too ashen and gray. It was at that moment that Ka'iulani noticed the odor of blood in the room. As she moved closer to her Aunty's bedside, she saw that the quilt blanket was matted down with blood. Knowing that Emma had so few days remaining, she didn't expect her to go this soon. Even as she was overcome by grief, she managed to call an ambulance first before contacting her Aunty Mae and her cousins, Thayer and Dianne.

Arrangements for Emma's services were made at Hawaiian Memorial Cemetery, where they would be held a month later at midday when the sun sat directly overhead and cast no shadow.

The funeral home exceeded its seating capacity. It was standing-room-only as people gathered within and without its walls. Flowers and wreaths were sent from numerous Hawaiian civic clubs and kanikapila groups that Emma belonged to. Even a letter of condolence was received from the Mayor's office where Emma had worked for many years. It was read as part of the eulogy that Mae delivered.

Mae recounted fond memories of her childhood with Emma and how Emma managed to keep her maiden name even after she married her late husband Henry. It was something unheard of during their era. Still, Emma never quite followed the norm and had a knack for doing things her way or, as Mae put it, "Emma was just po'o pa'akiki."

Thayer recounted his one and only "lickens" from his mother as the result of stealing candy from a local mom-and-pop store. Emma marched him back to the store the following day and offered the services of her son in whatever way possible to the store owners.

"It was embarrassing for my mom because the store owners were also my mom's classmates. Even after I raked their yard and washed their station wagon and fed their chickens on the first day, I still got lickens from my mom when I got home."

"But the part that Thayer forgot," Dianne said when her turn came to speak, "Is when Papa came home and found out from mom what Thayer did! He got worse lickens! I shouldn't talk, though, because all the lickens I got from Papa and Mom... I deserved every one. I was rotten. I really was."

Luther gave his ode of thanks to Emma as well, saying that it was Emma who helped Mae and himself to meet secretly when their parents had forbidden them to see each other. Luther was a boxer, and their parents did not approve.

"Emma Kaneuila," Dr. Reyes said, "Was the most hard-headed woman I've ever known. She drove me crazy because she would never listen to anything I told her, and it was utterly frustrating. But being so far away from my own home and missing my own parents, Emma always made sure that there was a place set for me at her dinner table whenever I felt homesick or whenever I just wanted to have some company. I've never felt such unconditional love from someone who expected nothing back except for your friendship. I'll miss the smile that Emma always gave me while she was busting my balls at the same time. There won't ever be anyone like her. I'm going to miss her. I'm going to miss her a lot."

After the eulogy, Kaʻiulani sang her Aunty Emma's favorite song, "Ua Like No A Like," which did not leave a dry eye in the house.

Emma also had friends in the United Japanese Society who attended her services and offered a lively Taiko drum performance from their youth group. Afterward, a young boy came forward and offered a song in his native language called "Haha Yo," meaning "Mother."

Emma's services reached such an uplifting crescendo that everyone forgot about the old woman's dire prediction concerning the thief who had stolen her lei niho palaoa. Toward the end, the funeral director announced only the immediate family would be allowed to remain to say their last goodbyes. All in attendance complied with the family's wishes.

A short time later, the pallbearers, Luther, Thayer, Richard, Dr. Reyes, and Dianne's two sons Haloa and Haluaola, were now ready to bring Emma's casket out to the hearse. Everything went smoothly and without incident. The vehicle brought Emma to the top of the hill, where she would be buried in an area facing the Koʻolau Mountains. The immediate family sat under the large green tent as Emma's casket was being brought to its final resting place.

Soon she would be lowered into the earth from whence she came.

Ka'iulani stood up and began to sing, "Ha'aheo e ka ua i na pali... ke nihi a'e la i ka nahele..."

Soon everyone joined in, "E 'uhai ana paha i ka liko... pua 'ahihi lehua o uka... aloha 'oe... aloha 'oe...e ke onaona noho i ka lipo... one fond embrace... a ho'i a'e au... until we meet again..."

Standing now as the casket was brought to where it would be placed on the hydraulic lift, the crowd of people wept openly after offering such a heartfelt tribute in song to the one person that meant so much to them and because of whom their lives would be a bit lonely now that she had passed into the realm of her ancestors.

A small gust of wind blew through the area as the pallbearers were just about to place the casket onto the lift. In the next second, another gust whipped suddenly through the gathering of people so fiercely that it knocked some of them off balance. The third gust was like an enormous fist toppling everything that was not nailed down. It stirred for a moment and ripped the green tent from the spikes, which, up until that moment, held the tent down firmly in the grass. The last gust of wind seemed to specifically whip itself around the pallbearers in a miniature tornado which caused blades of freshly mowed grass to blind them and throw them off balance.

Before they knew what was happening, the men dropped the casket on its left side just at the feet of where the immediate family was seated. The lid to the casket came off of its hinges and spilled Emma's body halfway onto the grass. Her head snapped suddenly to the left and caused her eyes to snap open. Everyone was horrified to see that Emma's eyes were staring directly at her older sister Mae. Everyone moved back for fear that whatever was going to happen to Mae might also happen to them if they were standing too close to her. No matter where Mae moved, her sister's eyes followed her. Mae screamed at the top of her lungs. Luther tried to grab her, but she kept pushing him away, screaming at him to leave her alone.

Torrents of rain suddenly fell, and thunder and lightning appeared practically out of nowhere. Mae only had a second to stop and look at the dark clouds that formed directly above her in the heavens. They seemed to be rolling furiously and developing into some kind of ominous shape. The crowd that was gathered there were witness to the unusual events that were transpiring in front of them. Now, a larger, darker shape formed in the clouds taking the guise of a man wearing a mahiʻole and an ahuʻula. Mae knew that it could only be one person.

Kaneuila. The god of lightning. She stood there frozen in fear as Kaneuila extended his right hand out to one cloud and then extended his left hand out to another cloud. From both of these, he gathered lightning in his palms. Looking directly at Mae, Kaneuila clapped both of his hands together and sent a searing bolt of lightning straight toward Mae, which split her right down the middle.

Instantly, she fell dead at Kaʻiulani's feet. The impact on hitting the ground almost caused Mae's body to slide off and separate into two pieces. The only thing preventing that from happening was Mae's shoulder purse slung across her chest, which served to hold her body together. The lighting had torn a gaping hole into the bottom of her purse, and there, as clear as day, everyone could see for themselves what the contents of Mae's shoulder purse were. It was the lei niho palaoa, fully intact and unharmed.

Later that evening, with Dr. Reyes to keep her company, Kaʻiulani read the letter that Aunty Emma instructed her to open only on the day after her funeral services.

Dearest Ka'iulani,

    If you are reading this letter, you must know that your Aunt Mae has been found out as the one who stole the lei niho palaoa and that, as of this writing, she is also dead. As I have said once before, the thief is a member of our household but is not blood family to us. There is a reason why the lei niho palaoa was given to me and not my older sister, Mae. She was not blood to us. She was adopted as a child and was never told about who she truly was per the instructions of our mother, Tutu Wawahilani. Our mother was a kind and gentle woman who believed in sparing the feelings of others. She never wanted Mae to feel like an outsider.

    After learning the truth, I felt I had to be kind to Mae and perhaps make her feel more important than ever. I did as much as I could so that she would never want for anything. We did not love Mae any less. This is why the lei niho palaoa could not be passed on to her, but it was never explained to her. I promised our mother I would not tell Mae. The lei niho palaoa was given to you because it's your blood right to have it.

    Please see to it that someone checks in on Luther now and again. Oh, how he must be suffering.

Remember how much I love you, my dearest Ka'iulani.

All My Love,

Aunty Emma

KALEPA

IT WAS 2:00 am AND THE phone rang for twenty-three minutes before Ben Makahi finally picked it up and answered the call.

"Aloha," Ben sighed.

"Ben Makahi?" the male voice asked.

"Yes," Ben replied.

"You don't know me," the voice said.

"Obviously."

"I apologize. My name is Larry Mendoza. I was born here in Honolulu, but I've lived in Pennsylvania for thirty years, and because of my job, I was able to move back here with my family ..."

"I'm sorry, Mr. Mendoza, but it's two in the morning, and I don't mean to be rude, but why do I care?" Ben interrupted.

"I hail from the Grand Lodge of Free and Accepted Masons of Pennsylvania," Larry Mendoza said, "I've traveled here from West to East, and I need you to listen to me."

"You're invoking the code?"

"Yes. It is your obligation."

"Gimme a second to get myself together, and I'll be right back. Hold on," Ben said.

"I don't have a second!" Larry said, raising his voice, "Every second is precious, please! Just listen to what I have to say!"

The sound of panic in Larry Mendoza's voice was enough to bring Ben out of his state of being less than half awake. It seemed that Ben Makahi's entire life was also in a state of being half awake and half asleep as well.

Although his daily life was filled with work, his Masonic duties to his lodge, and participating in hula and other cultural activities, he had just been going through the motions of existence but not really living. A year ago, his ex-wife won a bitter custody battle over their only child. Ben's daughter was the light of his life, and losing her in such a way came as a devastating blow. His ex-wife and daughter moved to the mainland to live with her new boyfriend. They had lived there all of two weeks when, one day, all three of them were killed in a head-on collision just a block away from their new home.

The bodies of both mother and daughter were flown home to Hawai'i for the services. The services at lower Nu'uanu Avenue couldn't continue as it took more than half the congregation at the Hosoi Mortuary to tear Ben away from his daughter's casket. Even then, he wouldn't leave the building until someone finally took drastic measures and knocked him out, and brought him home.

When the phone call came, Ben had no sympathy left in him for anything. Still, this present matter had to be urgent if another Freemason was invoking the code of obligation. Ben was bound by his Masonic oath to lend assistance in any way possible despite his personal circumstances. Fortunately, in this instance, it only required his undivided attention.

"Alright, alright," Ben agreed half-heartedly, "Go ahead."

"As I said," Larry continued, "This is urgent, but you have to hear the whole story, so it makes sense, okay?"

Ben had a feeling this was going to take a while. He got up to get a bottle of water from the fridge and replied, "Okay, I'm listening."

"So, I moved back home about a year ago, and I bought a nice, old house in Kapalama heights. It was built in the late 40s, and it had a nice. It had a nice, nostalgic feel to it, kind of warmth if you will. My wife and sons took to it right away, which helped with any moving anxiety that my family might have had. Things worked out smoothly for us, and I was amazed at how everything just seemed to fall into place. My wife Tisha got along great with everyone at her job, my job was the same, and my 16-year-old sons,

Ka'eo and Noa, had no problems at school. I really felt blessed, as if Hawai'i herself had been waiting for me all these years to return home. The one thing, the main thing, that I was really enthused about was getting back in touch with the Hawaiian side of my culture. So, every chance we had, my family and I would go to all the Hula shows and exhibits at the museums and the craft fairs and lectures. We even did the tourist thing for a while and went to the shows out in La'ie and Ko'olina and Campbell industrial park. It was cool, and I was lucky that Tisha and the boys supported my need to find cultural fulfillment because I know that they were at their limit at certain points, but they hung in there, you know?"

"About this time last year, I wanted to drive to the Pali Lookout. We saw it when we first moved here, but that was one of the places I wanted to spend more time at. It was a Saturday, and we all slept in a little later than usual. By the time I was ready to go, Tisha had sort of lost her enthusiasm for the drive. She suggested that the boys and I share some 'man time' together while she stayed at home and read a book. I wasn't gonna give her a hard time about it, I mean, she'd been a good sport all this time, and she deserved some time to herself. I promised her that we weren't going to be out too long and that I'd call her once we were done.

"It was already 4:45 pm when we left the house. When we hit the freeway from the Kalihi on-ramp, there was a traffic accident, so, as you can imagine, traffic was backed up for miles. I'm amazed that I can even remember the time now. Anyhow, all the while, my sons insisted that we just turn around and go back home or at least go see a movie or something, but I was stuck on going to the Pali lookout, and I wouldn't relent on the idea at all. It was 5:35 pm when we finally got to the Pali. The boys took everything in with the attention span of a starving man in a bakery. They were less than half-interested when I showed them the plaque at the lookout that depicted the ancient battle that took place there. Even the powerful winds that pushed them back up that slight incline didn't seem to pique their interest at all. They couldn't wait to get back to the car. Once we were back on the road, my wife called, and I put her on the Bluetooth overhead. She asked me if we were still at the Pali because the sun was going down.

The boys called out for their mom to meet us at the movies and buy the tickets before we got there.

"'What do you say, hun?' she asked me.

"I told her okay, and that we were on our way. Kaʻeo and Noa cheered. We'd gotten back out to the main highway when I noticed a turn-off to the left that was coming up. The sign said Nuʻuanu Pali Drive. I hadn't been down that road since I was in high school. My sons were freaking out, yelling at me about what I was doing and where was I going? I told Ka'eo to call Tisha and get her back on the Bluetooth. The phone only rang once when my wife picked up.

"She immediately asked what happened, and I explained that I just came across this place that I haven't seen since high school. I told her that we were going to take a quick look, and we'll be at the movies right after. I promised I would call her as soon as we were back in the car.

"The boys weren't happy about it, but my nostalgia won over any common sense I had that day. We used to drive down this road at night, telling each other ghost stories and looking for anything spooky. We got to an area just above the water reservoir, and I was pleasantly surprised to see that it was not only still there but that it hadn't changed much. It was about that time that something on the left side of the road caught my eye, and my eyes became affixed to what I saw. There was a little opening to what looked like a footpath that disappeared under the tall bamboo. If you blinked, you would have missed it for sure, and I have no doubt that many people probably have, but there it was. I pressed the brake and stared at it for a second. Ka'eo and Noa saw it too, and they asked me if it was some sort of trail. I said that it had to be and that we should go and check it out really quick. Even before they could protest, I had already parked the car and had them in tow right behind me as the three of us headed through the bushes. We were immediately greeted with the smell of ginger flowers. The plants grew taller than my head, and the scent was unmistakable. It was mixed in with the faint scent of earth and rotting vegetation as we made our way further into the dirt path. We were in the thick of a bamboo forest that blocked out most of the light directly above us. The wind that blew through the forest caused the bamboo to bang and scrape up against one another, and it made these unusual sounds that sort of made us nervous. Roots were sticking up out of the ground, which made the trek a little difficult, but we kept on until we discovered a different path to our left. It led up to another part of the bamboo forest, and it looked like it had been used a lot, so we weren't worried about getting lost at all. There were more roots and rocks along the way, but I'll tell you one thing for certain, what was at the end of that path was a big payoff. It was a dilapidated structure that, according to the plaque we read, belonged to Kamehameha the third. It was a quiet but breathtaking place. We were silent for a while as the three of us made our way into the structure and then just stood there and took it all in. It was really something in there, and I guess we got so caught up in the scenery so much that it suddenly got dark before we knew it. When I think about it now, I know it was my fault. We didn't have any flashlights or anything, and it was pitch black and very, very still. Nothing moved or made a sound. I told the boys that we were going to have to make it back down to the car purely by feel and that we'd have to hold on to one another and not panic.

"Our backs were facing the front entrance to this old home, so, as the three of us turned around to leave through that same entrance…" Larry paused for a few seconds.

"As we turned to leave," he continued, "There… there was… there was a long line of Hawaiian warriors blocking our way. They were all holding different types of weapons, and some were wearing feathered capes and helmets while others wore nothing but loincloths. I whispered to the boys that, on my count, we would make a run for the back entrance, but when I looked up, that door was blocked by another line of warriors as well. It's like we had cut off this procession right in the middle, and now we were stuck."

Ben sat there quietly with his cell phone next to his ear. He could tell that something big was coming and waited for Larry to continue without pushing him.

"One of them, the warriors, approached me, and it was really too dark to see his features, but he was tall and wide and looked like a seasoned warrior. I heard his voice in my head. He spoke to me in Hawaiian, and even though I only know a few words, for some odd reason, I could clearly understand what he was saying.

"He asked me if I saw any of my family members in that line of warriors. I looked at the warriors in front of us and the ones behind us. I hadn't recognized anyone, so I simply shook my head. The entire procession in front of us suddenly stepped aside as if they were allowing us to leave. I looked at my sons, and as they looked back at me. I simply motioned for them to follow me. That's the last thing I remembered. When I came to, I was sitting in the front seat of my car with my head down on the steering wheel. When I looked at my watch, it was 11:30 pm, but it couldn't have been! The last time I looked at my watch, it was 6:30! Kaʻeo and Noa were not there. I got out and ran up the trail a little. I called and called for them, but I got no answer. I must have driven up and down that road a million times with my highlights on, just screaming out their names before I finally called Tisha. When she answered the phone, she was pissed. While she was screaming at me on the phone, a thought that maybe Kaʻeo or Noa had called her. Maybe she came to get them, and they were now home with their mother listening to her yell at me as they sat there playing their Xbox. But when I glanced down at the passenger's seat next to me, their cell phones were right there. A chill suddenly crawled up my spine as I began to recall what just happened in the bamboo forest.

"I asked her, 'Tisha, the boys aren't at home with you, are they?'

"The tirade of swearing and screaming on the other side of the phone was astounding. I've never seen my wife so mad in all our years together. But I've never been this scared, either.

"I told her to get ready, that I was on my way home."

"Wait a minute!" Ben interrupted, "You're THAT Larry Mendoza? The guy whose two sons vanished up at Kaniakapupu? That Larry Mendoza?"

"Yeah," Larry replied, "I'm that guy."

"The authorities tried to say that you murdered your two sons and then disposed of the bodies, right? It was on the news for a while, and then all of a sudden, nobody heard anything about it anymore. I remember that. What happened?" Ben asked.

"I just told you what happened. If I had really committed murder, Ben, then you and I wouldn't be having this conversation because our Masonic laws would require you to turn me in. But I'm not a murderer. I wouldn't have been able to invoke the code if I had really killed Kaʻeo and Noa. Am I right?" Larry asked.

"So you're telling me that..." Ben began.

"Yes," Larry cut him off, "That's exactly what I'm telling you. My sons were taken by night marchers."

Ben needed a second to take in what he just heard.

"Hold on, hold on, wait a minute here. Is that what you told the authorities? Is this why this case just suddenly fell off the map?"

"Yes. As ridiculous as it sounds, that IS what happened, and I stuck to my story because it's the truth. Believe me, they ran all the tests, all the background checks, and they did all the prodding and poking down to the letter, and they came up with nothing. Inconclusive evidence, they said. So, they left me alone," Larry said.

"What about your wife?" Ben asked, "Did they do a number on her too?"

"No," Larry replied, "That same night when I went home to get my wife and took her to where I last saw my sons and told her the whole story, she didn't believe me. The look on her face was as if she were staring at a total stranger. There was a genuine fear in her eyes, and I knew at that moment that I'd lost her. When I called the police and they turned everything around on me as the number one suspect, it was too much for Tisha. She packed her things and went back to Pennsylvania.

"I was completely clueless as to what happened up at that place and how to deal with it. I had no idea that it was night marchers. Back then, I didn't even know what they were. Mind you, I didn't just lie down and die, although my insides were twisted twenty-four hours a day. I began to ask around and talk to people. At first, no one would help me once they heard my name. Many times people would just hang up their phones or slam the door in my face. It was tough, and I nearly gave up. Then one day, I was sitting at the food court in Ala Moana Shopping Center when one of the custodians walked up to me, a Hawaiian lady.

"She put her hand on my shoulder and gave me a serious look and said, 'I believe what you said on the news, sir. Too many things had happen up at that place where you and your sons went. Even the police know about that place, but they cannot come out and say that it's true. But everybody knows.'

"Everybody but me, I told her. I said that I don't even know what happened, and I wish someone would tell me, but no one wants to talk to me.

"She seemed surprised and asked me, 'No one told you?'

"I just shook my head. She let out a long sigh and took a seat right next to me, and looked me in the eye.

"'What happened to you,' she said, 'has happened to many people since the days of old in these islands. Your sons and you came across the travelers in the night, ka huaka'i hele i ka po, the night marchers.'

"Putting her finger up, the Hawaiian woman said to me, 'You have to listen so you can understand about what happened. Then, you can ask questions.'

"I nodded my head. I'd looked everywhere and searched for any information, so anything she had to say, I was open to.

"'The night marchers walk once a month during the phase of no moon, night or day, but they are mainly seen at night. Sometimes their torches are seen moving along the mountain ridges as they head down toward the ocean. Those who are unfortunate enough to be in their way, they suffered dire consequences. These men were warriors all their lives, and so, in the afterlife, they still perform the same duty, protecting the sacred Ali'i, the one they swore an everlasting allegiance to. But what had happen to you is different, no? "She said to me, 'What exactly had happen that night with your sons?'

"I told her what I told you. That one of the warriors asked me if I recognized any family members in the procession, and I said no. The entire rank and file stepped to one side to make room for us to leave or, at least, that's what I thought they were doing and, the next thing I know, I'm in my car.

"She was shaking her head, 'a life for a life.'

"'What do you mean?' I asked her.

"'The warrior asked you if you recognized any family members among their ranks because, if you did, if you had any ancestors in that procession, those ancestors would have come forward and called out your name and protected you. But since you had no family there to protect you, the night marchers took a life to replace a life. Two lives, in fact. That is also a tradition of the night marchers. That's all I can tell you.'

"Looking at the woman, I complained that none of what she just said told me how I could get my sons back.

"'There are many processions of night marchers. Each procession has its own night based on the moon phase. There are processions that are only meant for the gods, which cause terrible storms, and then there are the nights that belong to the ali'i, the chiefs.'

"She stared at me for a few more seconds as if she were searching for something.

"'Your mind is still haole even though a part of you is Hawaiian. On your mama's side, no?'

"I answered yes and asked her how she knew that.

"'Because you ask too many questions and you haven't heard anything that I have just told you. Hopefully, the Hawaiian side of you has absorbed what I've said into the pores of your skin, and maybe it will reach out to you in your dreams. Let's pray that this is what will happen. For a parent who loves their children so much and then they lose them without knowing what happened to them, is the worst suffering. Akua knows I would have given my own life for my child if anything like that ever happened to me. It wouldn't have been a second thought.

"The woman gave me a big hug and, when she walked away, she simply disappeared into the crowd of people in the food court. The second I got home to my big, empty house, I just crashed on the couch."

There was a few seconds of silence on the other side of the phone, and Larry asked, "Ben? Ben, are you still there?"

"I'm here," Ben said, "go on."

"Okay," Larry continued, "It turns out that the woman was right. What she said did sink in. I dreamt the whole thing back again, the meeting in the food court with that Hawaiian woman and the way she sat in front of me and talkod, except it kept playing itself back in fragments, and certain parts of our conversation would repeat itself back in the dream over and over again."

"What part was that?" Ben asked.

"The part about certain processions having their own night," Larry answered, "It kept repeating itself over and over again in my dream until I finally got the message. The next day, I began researching the Hawaiian moon phases, and I got as much information online as I could gather regarding the night marchers. A lot of it was just urban legend BS, but one bit of information rang true. I found it on a blog of all things. It talked about a man who mysteriously lost his brother in Kahana valley while hiking. The man claimed that they encountered a night marcher procession in broad daylight and that his brother disappeared. That's all there was to the blog, just that short blurb and nothing else. I emailed the owner of the blog site for any information that he might have concerning the man in the story. I sort of fudged the truth and told him that my uncle had had a similar experience and that I just wanted to meet the guy and compare the information. A day later, I got a reply. It was an address for a guy named Travis Kaneakua out in Waiahole.

"By that afternoon, I was driving up the road when I saw the address on an old, beat-up mailbox. There was a dirt road right behind it lined with tall grass, and stray dogs were milling about here and there on the path. They paid no attention to my truck and went on about their business. At the very end of this dirt road was a Quonset hut that sat under the shade of a huge mango tree. I walked up to the porch, and the steps creaked so loud that if Travis wasn't aware of my presence beforehand, he was now. I didn't even get a chance to knock on the screen door when it opened, and out stepped a Hawaiian man about my height and build. He had short white hair and a white beard that was still growing in. He was dressed in a white t-shirt and gray shorts. His eyes were intense as he looked me over, and you can imagine my surprise when he called me by my name!

"I was taken aback for a second before I replied, asking how he knew.

"He said that my email address is 'larry_m,' and it didn't take his son long to figure it out. Smart kid. His kid is about the same age as my boys.

"I said, 'You know about me?' And at that point, I began to understand what the Hawaiian lady meant by asking too many questions. I just shut my mouth and listened.

"He said, 'Yeah, I know about you, brah. We have something in common. Kinda makes sense that you wen come here. You like know what happened to me and my braddah, right?'

"I said, 'Yes if you don't mind, I'd like to know.'

"He told me it was 2004. He and his brother were hiking in the back of Kahana Valley. All of a sudden, they saw a huge army of Hawaiian warriors coming. By then, it was too late. The warriors just showed up out of nowhere.

"Travis paused at this point, and tears flowed freely down his cheeks.

"He said they stripped down naked and lay flat on the ground, but that didn't work. Two of the night marchers came out of the line and grabbed Travis and were going to take him with them. Then he says his brother started yelling over and over, 'Kalepa! Kalepa! Kalepa!'

Travis went silent after that and didn't say anything more.

"I spoke up then, 'They intended to take you? But what was it that your brother was saying? Kalepa?'

"Travis said, 'Braddah, you go find out what Kalepa means and, once you find that out, then you ask yourself if that's what you really willing to do?'

"With that, Travis turned around and went back into his house."

On the other end of the telephone connection, Ben's world opened up when he, too, heard the word Kalepa. Keeping Larry on the phone, Ben began to get dressed. He went to the bathroom, rinsed his mouth out with some

Listerine, and then went to his computer. Ben sent an email to his ex–sister–in–law and cc'd his friend Dennis Ching. Instinct told Ben where to find Larry, and it was that same instinct that pushed him out the front door and into his car.

"So," Ben asked, "did you do your research? What did you come up with?"

"Well," Larry replied, "this is where I ask you about my brother master mason's secret as your own."

"I understand," Ben replied, "begin the code."

The code was just what Ben needed. It bought him the necessary time required to keep Larry on the phone while Ben sped through the night in order to get to where he knew Larry Mendoza was at that moment. The code was lengthy, and it was just Ben's luck that Larry knew the code in its long–form. More time bought! Passing the University off–ramp, Ben realized that he and Larry were midway through the code. Masonic tradition said that the code could not be interrupted, so he couldn't pretend that he had a hard time hearing Larry. Instead, he drove faster.

By the time Ben was heading up the Pali Highway, the code was nearing its completion when the phone suddenly went dead. All Ben could do now was drive faster and buy time. He passed the right turn to the Nuʻuanu Pali Drive and headed up further to where the road came out again on the main highway, and drove back down the road from the top. Just above the water reservoir is where Ben saw the white Ford F150 parked facing the other direction. He immediately made a U-turn and parked right behind what he knew to be Larry's truck.

Taking his flashlight out of his glove compartment, Ben dashed out of his car and sped off into the dark bamboo forest as fast as he could. He knew this trail like the back of his hand. He'd spent many afternoons at the abandoned mansion with his daughter having picnics or looking for bugs. Now his feet told the rest of his body where to go as they had become familiar with the terrain as well. The wind whipped the canopy of the bamboo forest wildly and made it sound like traffic on a highway going through the area.

Finally reaching Kaniakapupu itself, Ben saw that everything was now dead-quiet. He also saw the long procession of night marcher torches coming from the deep forest, going through the mansion's back door, and then coming out of the front. Time was of the essence, and there was no room for protocol. Running into the side door of Kauikeaouli's mansion, Ben stopped dead in his tracks. In the center of the open structure, he saw Larry Mendoza standing face-to-face with a warrior from the line. There wasn't a moment left to think, and Ben had to act quickly.

"Kalepa! Kalepa! Kalepa!" Ben screamed.

Larry and the entire procession of night marchers turned to look in Ben's direction. With his whole body bent in deference to the fierce warriors before him, Ben stated his case.

"He kalepa keia e na kupuna ha'aheo... he noi kalepa keia! 'O au 'o Makahi mai ka moku 'o keawe, mai ke kumu la'au nui o tu'u mau kupuna aloha. He kalepa keia e na pu'ali koa! 'Oi aku ka waiwai o ku'u kino ma mua o neia kanaka hapa Hawai'i me kana keiki kane 'elua! He noi kalepa keia! 'O au kau kama! E lawe mai ia'u!"

"What are you doing?" Larry hissed at him.

"Shut up," Ben said quietly, "Don't say anything more. Just shut up."

The head warrior looked back at the rest of the procession for approval, to which they nodded in the affirmative. The warrior himself then nodded and stepped to the side. As Ben Makahi stepped into the procession, Ka'eo and Noa Mendoza stepped out and joined their father at his side.

"What are you doing?" Larry shouted, "This was my fight, not yours! You were supposed to honor the code and take my sons back home to their mother! I flew her back here and told her to wait at our house! This is not the code!"

"This IS the code," Ben said, "You were going to make the ultimate sacrifice as a father and give your life in exchange for the lives of your sons. But I make the ultimate sacrifice as a Freemason and give my life in order to protect you and your family. That's also part of the code. Now get out of here before these guys change their minds. Go!"

"Ben, Ben...I...." Larry couldn't get the words out, but Ben Makahi's eyes told him that he understood what Larry wanted to say.

"Go, Larry," Ben said as he gestured to Larry's sons, "go, live."

As the ghostly line began to move, Ben saw a familiar face that gave him cause to smile. His little daughter's hand reached out and held his own as they now stood side by side. Before Larry could say anything more, the entire procession vanished right in front of him. He held on to Ka'eo and Noa and cried tears of joy and relief. While heading down the trail, Larry Mendoza promised his sons that he would explain everything and that he wanted to hear about everything that happened to them.

The porch light at the Kapalama house lit Larry Mendoza's face just enough so that Tisha could see him sitting on his rocking chair. Silently, she joined him as she sat on his lap and hugged him. Ka'eo and Noa were just inside the living room, fast asleep on the sofas. Somewhere in the distance, Larry thought that he heard the sound of pahu drums, which made him jump out of his seat. Much to his surprise, it was just a modified sedan with speakers thumping out the downbeat to Cypress Hill's anthem of angst, "Jump."

Without his daughter's presence in his life, Ben Makahi felt that there was no purpose for him in the living world. The night he left to find Larry Mendoza, Ben emailed his last will and testament to his ex-sister-in-law and his friend, Dennis Ching, who was also Ben's attorney. Now, on the night of Kane, which falls but once a month, Ben and his daughter traverse the old trail with a thousand other warriors of their family line. Perhaps Ben might be seen again, but it will be under the cover of a moonless night that is only lit up by the glow of thousands of torch lights as they march from the Ko'olau mountains all the way down to the sea.

TEDDY

THE DAY CAME LIKE ANY other as the sun rose in the east and set its light through the windows of Alan Higashi's home. It was the sunlight that woke Alan from his sleep when it invaded his living room and caused him to be roused from his couch without a thought. As his vision came into focus, he was surprised to see his ex-girlfriend Kenzie fast asleep on the carpeted floor at the foot of his couch."

"Oh yeah," he said to himself with sarcasm, "How could I forget?"

Kenzie and Alan had been broken up for a while, at least in Alan's mind they had. She would still have one of her incidents where she would randomly show up unannounced at Alan's apartment and start to beg him to take her back. It usually ended with Kenzie threatening to commit suicide once she realized that Alan wasn't going to budge. Last night was a bit different. Kenzie was just too tired to argue and needed somewhere to crash. Alan stepped over her sleeping form and headed to the bathroom to get ready for work. Another trek through midtown traffic just to get to a job that wasn't going to give any one of its employees a raise. They were all told that they could put up with it or leave. So, why was Alan still there after five years?

"Nothing else better out there," he growled to himself in the mirror. Stepping into the shower now, he turned the water up to full blast and set it on cold. It's the only thing that could clear the cobwebs out of his head and help make him conscious for the rest of the day.

His clothing choice always consisted of a buttoned–down, long–sleeved shirt, usually in green or olive drab, a pair of khaki slacks, and hiking boots. With that came his shoulder bag, which carried his laptop and five packets of jasmine tea that he saved for lunch.

Lunch itself came from the Mediterranean Cafe a block away from his office. He always ordered whatever the cashier recommended because he had a crush on her. He couldn't pronounce her name, but, nevertheless, he was haunted by her sharp, gray–colored eyes and her raspy voice. Her hair fell about her shoulders in natural curls. Alan could only imagine that in another life, she must have been Scheherazade. He must have been the king who found himself seduced by her nightly tales of romance and wonder.

That and the fact that Alan's boss was a dog lover and allowed Alan to bring his dog to work with him were the only things that made the day worthwhile. Teddy, Alan's golden retriever, was the office mascot. Whenever Teddy needed to go outside, he would always walk toward the main door and sit there; it was Teddy's periodic signal for potty time. If Alan was too busy trying to get a report done, there was always someone else in the office who loved taking Teddy outside for his walk since it gave them a bit of a break as well.

The morning went the way it usually did; traffic was a bear for forty minutes into town, and that was only from Makiki Heights. Alan parked in his usual space just behind the old MacDonald's off of Queen and Bishop Streets. The elevator ride to his third-floor office was also the same ride with the same people going to their individual floors to fill in a day of work. The same Ultra Man toys decorated Alan's desk and a slightly fading picture of himself and Kelly Hu that was taken at a mandatory fundraiser put on by his boss at Lau Yee Chai. The scotch tape that held the image to the edge of Alan's computer screen was beginning to come loose.

"Why Kelly?" Alan asked, "Why now? Why couldn't you have just hung on instead of making me tape you back on again?"

Taking a short pair of scissors from his desk drawer, he cut off the old scotch tape from the top of the small photograph and replaced it with a pushpin. Sticking the miniature portrait onto his mini bulletin board.

"You see, Kelly?" Alan said in a deadpan voice, "I didn't want to push the issue, but you left me no choice. What could I do, babe? My hands are tied."

Leaning outside of the miniature wall of his small cubicle, Alan's workmate Piker piped up, "I'm starting to worry about you and Kelly. Sounds like it's starting to get physical. Maybe I should tell your middle eastern girlfriend about your abusive habits?"

Alan's reply came in a wadded-up ball of Post-Its with tape wrapped around it, sticky side out. It landed in Piker's orange, curly afro and dangled there like a Christmas ornament.

"Haha, Higashi. Piker will have his revenge!"

Along with Teddy, Alan Higashi and Piker Teruya were always the first to take their lunch hour together. Piker was the only hapa kid Alan knew whose facial features looked more like his Japanese father than his Irish mother, except that he had orange hair and freckles on his cheeks. Even among his own people, Piker looked so unique that no one knew what to make of him. Rather than make fun of Piker, they treated him more like a celebrity. The special treatment he received nover went to his head. But, whatever benefits he may have derived from his status,

Piker always made sure that his best friend, Alan Higashi, shared in the glory as well. However, on days like this, it was Alan's chance for glory as they neared his favorite place to eat.

For Piker, the novelty of the daily outing to the Mediterranean Café had worn out for him very early on. It was painful for him to watch Alan make a complete fool of himself to impress a girl who really didn't want to have anything to do with him. So, Piker and Teddy would head to the Subway shop or the Pork Adobo place on Fort Street Mall instead. Teddy loved Pork Adobo, but, as a result, Alan was the one who had to suffer the consequences at home later on. Piker would always get an earful over the phone. After a few minutes of yelling, an exchange of colorful descriptions of each other's mothers followed.

Piker would then say, "Oh hey, my dad says we're having Wafu Steak, rice, natto, and chicken furikake. He said, come over and eat."

Before Alan could even politely refuse the invite, Piker's father would get on the phone to put in his two cents, "Alan?"

Piker's father was a great businessman at a local car dealership. Still, he came off more like a samurai general leading his warriors into battle.

124

"Hi, Mr. Teruya," Alan replied.

"Eh, we get pahleeeenty food you! Come here now and eat before all gone."

There was no refusing Mr. Dean Teruya. He never took "no" for an answer.

Alan and Piker were only halfway to the little shopping complex when Teddy began to put up a big fuss and refused to go any further. Quite unusual for Teddy as he was always the first one into the little shopping complex. The owners of each individual store always gave Teddy a warm greeting or a wave. Today, however, Teddy suddenly refused to take another step forward. There was no whimpering or crying but, instead, a low growl as if there were something in the building he was afraid of. Teddy's ears were down, and his tail was tucked between his legs. He didn't even bother to bark but slowly backed up to the sidewalk. He suddenly defecated and urinated at the same time.

Alan didn't know what to make of it, "He's afraid of something. What's wrong, Teddy? What's got you so spooked?"

Alan got no reply of any kind. Teddy just looked at the opening to the complex and continued to growl and bared his teeth.

"What's wrong with him, Al? I've never seen him like this," Piker asked.

"I don't know," Alan replied, "He's acting weird. Listen, I'll stay with him. Why don't you go get your food, and when you get back, I'll go get my food, and you can watch him."

"Are you sure?" Piker smiled, "You don't want to miss your quality time with you know who?"

"Yeah, no worries," Alan waved him off, "Go, go..."

However, the second Piker began to leave, Teddy leaped forward, grabbed Piker's pant leg with his teeth, and dragged him back. Teddy instantly let go and barked at Piker three times and then went right back to staring at the building and growling.

"Alright," Piker said, "Your dog has officially gone, *Cujo!*"

"Teddy, what's wrong with you?" Alan was yelling at the dog now, "That's Piker! You know Piker! Listen, you stay with him. I'll go in. I'll be right back."

In an instant, Teddy stood on his hind legs, placed his paws on Alan's chest, and gave him a low, threatening growl. All the while baring his teeth and nearly salivating on his owner's shirt, Teddy refused to let Alan and Piker leave the sidewalk and go into the building. Alan was furious.

126

"Teddy godammit, you frickin' dog!"

The retriever held his ground and backed the two men up to the edge of the sidewalk.

Yulianna and her family thought they had seen the last of their home country near the Carpathian Mountains and its evil lineage. They saw the need to move after seeing their kind being sensationalized in the movies. It wasn't safe anymore. It was easy to hide behind the myth and allegory of who the uneducated public thought they were in the early days. Still, Hollywood made it impossible for them to exist in privacy. Their covert exodus to Serbia in 1995 was supposed to have been their liberation from their past. It was hoped that they could have the everyday life that they collectively longed for.

In 1995, what proved to be their undoing was the ethnic cleansing campaign carried out by the Bosnian Serb forces in Srebrenica. More than seven thousand Bosnian Muslims, mainly men, and boys, were killed. Their kind practiced secrecy and strict adherence to a discipline almost at a level of fanaticism. The carnage, however, and the number of corpses proved to be too much for the weaker of their kind. They came in droves and fed so voraciously without regard to the consequences that they became easy targets for those who hunted them.

The elder of their kind waited and bided their time, partaking wisely and not gorging themselves needlessly. They took what they needed and left as quickly as they came, but it was too late in this instance. The younger and more foolish of Yulianna's family exposed the rest and gave away their lair's location. The hunters simply let them feed and, when the foolish ones were done, they followed them home. The second their nest was found, more hunters came and wiped them out. Only a lucky few escaped, and those few would prove to be a burden on their human families.

Being a bustling city and a melting pot of many ethnicities, Honolulu seemed to be the logical choice for Yulianna and her clan. It would be easy for them to blend in. As he came to be known, her grandfather's eldest brother Alexandru or Papa Dru moved to the islands in the late 1950s to make a new life for himself. He had wanted to see the world that existed beyond Romania and managed to stow away on a steamship headed for America. No ticket meant there was no one to coerce into revealing where he went.

His stay in the bowels of the ship was cramped and uncomfortable. The bread and sausage that Alexandru brought with him for the journey didn't last very long. The smell of iron and fuel made his empty stomach turn. His arrival in New York went unnoticed and, with some old family gold that he was able to sell, he rented a small apartment. He had quickly found that the smell of death was too overwhelming, too much of a reminder of home, and decided that his stay in New York would not be for very long.

Learning that there were opportunities on the West Coast, Alexandru boarded a train headed for San Francisco. He found that the underlying stench of San Francisco was similar to that of New York. However, it was here that he discovered tales of an island paradise that was young and fresh. He used what was left of his gold to purchase a first–class ticket on the SS Lurline bound for Honolulu.

When he stepped off the gangplank at Aloha Tower's pier, Alexandru felt he had come home. This is where he would stay for the rest of his life, never feeling the need to leave. He found odd jobs here and there, but after tooling around for a few months, he found a job working for E.K. Fernandez. Soon after, he met Al Karasick, who was putting together a local professional wrestling promotion in Honolulu. Alexandru was only seventeen at the time, and someone like Al, who was bigger than life to a boy at such a young age, would prove to be a good influence on him. Karasick had also taught the boy how to speak English, and his student proved to be a quick study. Alexandru plied his trade in the wrestling business as a journeyman wrestler who paid his dues by doing jobs for other wrestlers who were top stars or up-and-comers. Often Alexandru worked under a mask and was known as the Masked Killer, a heel or bad guy.

One night, while working a stiff match with a young Nick Bockwinkle, Alexandru suddenly felt a chill crawl up his spine, and it stopped him dead in his tracks. It was something he hadn't felt since he was a child growing up in the Carpathian Mountains of Romania. It seemed impossible that one of his kind that his clan was charged to care for could have found his way here to Honolulu from the other side of the world. Yet, there he was, sitting in the third row. Dressed in a pin-striped suit and tie with a pair of spats, he was out of place amongst the mixed crowd of Hawaiians and other locals dressed in aloha shirts or Bermuda shorts. It was Decebal.

His name meant "stronger than ten," which he probably was. He hadn't aged a day since Alexandru last saw him when he was only ten years old. There was no expression on his face, only the impression that he wanted Alexandru to be aware of his presence. For that split second that Alexandru was distracted, Nick Bockwinkle grabbed the young boy by the head and threw him to the mat for a snap mare, applied a shoot headlock, and put Dru to sleep.

Later on, after Al Karasick paid Alexandru his fee for the night, he grabbed his overcoat and made his way out of the front door of the Civic Auditorium. This was against the rules for anyone in the wrestling business because it was essential to keep the business tight. But even more importantly, the talent always left through the back of the house. Going through the front door meant that you broke Kayfabe, one of the more sacred and unspoken business rules. Alexandru was unconcerned since he wrestled under a mask, and there would have been no way that any fan could make him on the spot. He quickly crossed South King Street and made his way down Keʻeaumoku Street to Likelike Drive Inn for a quick meal. In the dark parking lot, Alexandru was not surprised when he heard the voice from behind him.

"Sunt dezamăgit," came Decebal's grainy voice.

"Why are you disappointed?" the young man asked.

"Tu vorbeşti Engleză?" he inquired.

"Yes," Alexandru said, "I speak English. Why are you disappointed?"

"Ai putea fi ucis ca omul cu uşurinţă. Puteţi să–l bate. Au uitat de unde ai venit? You could have killed that man easily. But you let him beat you. Have you forgotten where you come from?"

Decebal kept his eyes focused straight ahead without looking at Alexandru once. There was a smile on his face that didn't necessarily mean he was happy.

"Acest lucru fac este configurat. Aceasta nu este real. Mister Karasick este un om bun. El ma trateaza ca pe propriul fiu. Când îmi spune să fac ceva, o fac. Eu nu plâng și am ține gura închisă." Alexandru explained, "It's set up. It's not meant to be real. Mister Karasick is good to me. He treats me like his own son. When he asks me to do something, I do it. I don't complain."

"Alexandru," Decebal began, "Poate că acest loc a avut o influenta proasta asupra ta? Perhaps this place has had a bad influence on your mind?"

"Listen to me, Decebal," the boy continued, "This place, these Hawaiian people, they are not like people from anywhere else in the world. Their hearts are pure. They take you in and feed you because it is considered bad manners if they don't. They give without expecting anything back, and yet they have had so much taken away from them. If this is what you consider to be a bad influence, then perhaps I am already corrupted."

Now Decebal's eyes met Alexandru's eyes straight on, "Do you know that there are some of our kind here in

Honolulu? They are from the Philippines. They are called Aswang. Filthy creatures. These Hawaiian people have their guardian deities who take the form of sharks and other animals. The gods that they once worshipped are still here, and they are not aware of it in the least. Or they must be afraid. It is a strange language they have. The locals here speak another dialect of English. The words are almost arranged backward."

"It's called Pidgin. Why are you here, Decebal?" Alexandru was almost irritated at the presence of this abomination he was supposed to revere as blood.

"Some of the Hawaiian people still revere their old gods. I thought perhaps that I could make use of that old pagan practice. What do you think?" Decebal laughed now even more heartily, "We could be gods here, Alexandru. They would fear us. Our power over this place would be unlimited. We could use their own superstitions to suppress them and make them our slaves."

Brave beyond his years, Alexandru now stood face to face with something that had lived longer than he had and indeed had the strength of ten men. But the young boy had no concern for his own life. There was something about Hawai'i that cleansed his heart and gave him peace of mind. It was something that he instinctively wanted to protect at all costs. Even if it meant killing one of his own.

"After everything we've done to protect elders like yourselves, from the hunters and priests and fanatics and Nazis, you want to come here and create your own Olympus? You want to subjugate a race of people and become their god? Do you know what that will bring to this place? We may be a world away from our home, but word will get out, and the hunters will find you, and there won't be anything that I can do to protect you. I'm sorry, Decebal. I won't let you do it."

Decebal was stunned at the boy's disobedience. He had to be taught a lesson. He lifted the boy off of the ground by his throat without effort, his sharp fangs bare.

"Blood, you are! You will obey your code to feed us who are damned, or you will be damned! Do you understand, boy?" Decebal's eyes were now blood-red and filled with the fury of hell itself.

"Fii atent. Suntem într-un loc public..." Alexandru now struggled to speak under Decebal's iron grip around his throat, "Be Careful... we are in a public place."

Realizing the truth of what the boy said, Decebal let him go. Ke'eaumoku street was bustling with traffic. He quickly fixed his coat and tie and made sure that no one saw what just happened. That was the moment that Alexandru needed.

134

He depended on elders like Decebal, who still held on to the old ways and demanded respect. His open disregard worked. Alexandru knew that he could not accomplish what he needed to do with a free attack. A slight on Decebal's ego would have to do the trick, and it worked. In one swift motion, the young man drew the short, silver, jeweled sword from his coat. Using his hips for momentum, he swung the blade in a short arc and decapitated his elder's head from the rest of his body. Without a second to waste, Alexandru quickly wrapped Decebal's head in his overcoat and hid his body behind some garbage cans. The meal would have to wait.

Alexandru ran back up Ke'eaumoku Street, made his way across Beretania, and headed toward Makiki and Kinau Streets to the Masonic Temple. The parking lot was full and, with the lights on upstairs and all of the doors closed downstairs, it meant that all of the Freemasons were busy conducting their rituals, and they would not come out for a long while.

Alexandru found a little alley behind the Masonic temple, and it was there that he managed to bury Decebal's head. He would have to return for the body later and take it to the incinerator at Kaka'ako. The code from the old country was antiquated and had no place in Hawai'i. It was too precious to be defiled by Decebal or any other elder who dared to make this town their personal feeding ground. On that day, Alexandru promised himself that he would be Hawaii's personal protector of his own kind.

The Elders. Not many came but, when they did, Alexandru would find them and rid the islands of them before they could spread their evil in his paradise.

In late 1996, when Yulianna's family arrived, Alexandru was happy to see his youngest brother Andrei and Andrei's wife, Alina. He embraced his brother warmly and shed tears of happiness.

"Aloha," he said to his brother. He greeted each of his family members the same way. The gesture itself was very awkward and out of character for anyone from Romania. Alexandru had lived in Hawai'i for so long that he had found the ancient customs were too conservative for his tastes.

He was also relieved to find that there were no elders among them. His heart, however, was made warm when he saw his niece, Miruna, and her husband, Vasile. Holding Miruna's hand was her ten-year-old daughter, Yulianna.

The girl worked the lunch shift while standing nervously at her cash register. Try as she might, she couldn't take her mind off of the large crate that arrived late last night. Her mother was yelling at her now as the line of customers got longer. She noticed that the digital clock next to the register read 12:10 p.m. The strange Japanese boy wasn't in line. For a second, she found it to be unusual. He never missed a day. He was bothersome but always polite. For some reason, she wished he were here; there was an honest look to him that she liked.

Most of the men who stood in her line only came to look at her and to think unsavory thoughts. It was easy to read their eyes. Her grandmother had taught her well to read deeply into the eyes of human beings, for it would reveal their true intent. The intent in the eyes of the strange Japanese boy was only that of trust and perhaps more, but the girl couldn't afford to get close to anyone, much less make friends. In her heart, she felt that it was too costly. Especially with the circumstances regarding the arrival of the enormous crate, the worry increased ten–fold. It was just after three in the morning when the girl and her family drove down to the docks to pick up the crate and bring it home.

On the second floor, it was directly above where the girl now stood as she worked the cash register, servicing customers. It contained an oversized casket. In it lay the body of her uncle. She dreaded the end of the day when she would have to see the sunset in the west. It meant that her uncle would be awake, and he would be hungry. Where was Papa Dru? She had hoped that he would have arrived early, but no one has seen him yet. Time was getting short.

Alan and Piker quickly brought Teddy back to the office. They left him there, returning to the little shopping complex when they were sure Teddy was okay. Piker headed straight to Subway while Alan walked to the Mediterranean Café and took his place at the line's back. He glanced up toward the front of the line and saw that the girl was smiling at him. Alan looked around to make sure that she wasn't extending salutations to someone else. It would be pretty embarrassing if he waved back only to find out that the greetings were not his. But he wasn't mistaken; the girl was looking directly at him and waved him to the front. He went with a bit of hesitation and nervousness.

"Hi, I'm Alan," he extended his hand. The girl took his hand and held on to it instead of shaking it. Her touch was very soft. Alan could feel himself getting a bit flush.

"I'm Yulianna. You can stand here and keep me company while my grandmother makes your favorite dish," she smiled at him, and Alan found himself riveted to the spot. He wondered how Yulianna's grandmother knew what his favorite dish was.

Oh, yeah, he thought to himself, it's probably because I order the same thing all the time.

Piker bit into his Italian BMT sandwich and headed to the Mediterranean Café to wait for Alan. His mind kept going back to Teddy and his strange aggressive behavior. The second they took Teddy back to the office, he was fine. He was right back to his usual self, and his happy-go-lucky demeanor reappeared as if nothing happened. Piker couldn't figure it out.

Two blocks away in Alan's office, Teddy could hear an unfamiliar voice call his name again and again. The voice invaded his thoughts, and he didn't like it. He didn't like the smell that came with it.

"Teddy," the voice said, "Teddy, I know you can hear me. Be a good dog and keep away from this place. I will bring harm to your friends if you do not heed my warning."

Teddy's thoughts replied to the strange voice, "The man and his friend are mines. I will protect them from your harm. You will not do this thing that you say. I will not let you. You are not a man. You are something evil."

The voice in Teddy's thoughts simply laughed.

Teddy laid his head on his paws and waited for Alan to return. He was afraid for his man and his friend.

Alina came to the cash register to retrieve Alan and had him sit at a small table near the kitchen. She served him a plate of his favorite dish, a falafel with a kabob on the side, and substantial potato slices with a dab of hummus.

"Eat," she said to Alan as she brought him a tall glass of his favorite home-squeezed lemonade that he always ordered, "Yulianna says you are a good boy. I hope she is right, yes?"

"Uh, yes," Alan hesitated. With that, the old woman retreated to the kitchen to continue cooking. Alan couldn't figure out what was going on. One day Yulianna wouldn't give him the time of day, and the next day he's suddenly treated like family. What changed?

Just then, a huge burly man with his dark hair pulled back into a ponytail walked into the Café. He looked at Yulianna and pointed toward the kitchen as he continued on.

"When the lunch line dies down, we all have to talk."

"Yes, Papa Dru," the girl was finally relieved.

Walking past Alan, he gently tapped him on the shoulder with his huge meaty hands and extended a warm greeting, "Aloha, my friend! I'm Papa Dru." Alan's right hand practically disappeared in Papa Dru's hand altogether.

Standing up now and putting his plate aside, Alan returned the salutation, "Aloha! I'm Alan."

"Sit," Papa Dru said, "Don't let me interrupt your meal. Please eat."

"Mahalo," Alan replied.

Walking into the café, Piker was pleasantly surprised to see where Alan was sitting and pulled up a chair right in front of him.

"Okay," Piker said, "How did you suddenly get to sit next to the kitchen? Yesterday you were relegated to standing in line like everybody else, for the Falafel Nazi! And then, what is the deal with your retriever?"

"Dunno," Alan said, "I've never seen Teddy like that. He was really freaked out, but over what? I can't say."

"I think my family can answer that question for you," Yulianna suddenly interrupted, "Will you come to the kitchen and join us, the both of you? My family would like to talk with you."

Alan didn't know what to think. This was all so sudden.

"I knew it!" Piker said, "All this special treatment couldn't have been a random act of kindness! This is gonna be like one of those *Saw* movies! They're gonna take us in the back and chop us up to bits, but slowly, while we're still awake and with no anesthesia!"

Papa Dru peaked out of the kitchen and smiled, "Hele mai 'olua, please join us." The invitation was sincere, and there was no way to avoid such kindness from a man who was three times their size.

Alan and Piker followed Yulianna into the kitchen. They found her family gathered around a big circular table at the opposite end. She introduced her family to her two new friends.

"This is my Grandfather, Andrei, and my grandmother, Alina. My Papa Dru or Alexandru, my grand uncle. My father, Vasile, and my mother, Miruna."

Everyone bowed and smiled gently at the two young men. The people who stood before Alan were very handsome people who seemed to have led a prosperous and healthy life. It radiated from them like sunlight. But there was also some concern in their demeanor. For some reason, Alan and Piker sensed that it had to do with them.

"Please," Andrei insisted, "Sit. We only need a minute of your time."

As soon as the two young men were seated, Papa Dru, the oldest male in the clan, spoke. "There are many formalities that we would normally have to observe but, considering the circumstances, we are going to forego our usual customs and get straight to the point."

Alan and Piker sat there dumbfounded and had no clue as to what was going on. Andrei gave the nod to his granddaughter.

"Where did you get your dog from?" Yulianna asked.

"Teddy?" Alan asked, "Uh, I got Teddy when he was about two years old. I found him wandering around outside the emergency room at Straub Hospital. He actually followed me home. We've been pals ever since," Alan looked around the table at Yulianna's family, "Is there a problem with Teddy? Do you not want me to bring him around anymore?"

"No," Andrei said, "There is nothing wrong with your dog. In fact, we believe he is special. Because of that, we also believe that he may be in danger and that the two of you may be in danger as well."

"I told you!" Piker whispered through his teeth, "*Saw!*"

"Shut up!" Alan hushed him. He looked into the eyes of each of Yulianna's family members one by one. He could see that this was not a joke or some prank that Piker must have dreamed up.

"Hold on. Are you guys serious? This is... this is all too strange. You're seriously saying that something is wrong with my retriever and that Piker and I are in danger? Really?"

"We understand that this is confusing for you and so sudden. It may be too much to take in," Andrei said, "Yulianna will walk you back to your office and explain everything. Thank you for talking to us."

With that, the family excused themselves and set about doing their regular after–lunch clean–up. Yulianna put her apron away and led Alan and Piker out of the café.

"I don't have time to go into details," Yulianna began, "So I'm just going to give it to you straight. For as long as I can remember, my family has been charged with hiding our elders' secrecy from men called Hunters so that they would not be found out and killed. We were supposed to help feed the elders as well."

"So, you had to keep senior citizens in your family safe from people who were hunting them down? What did these elders do that was so bad?" Piker asked.

"You talk too much, and you don't listen enough," Yulianna told Piker. Looking at Alan, she continued, "They are vampires. The care of them sometimes can be too much of a burden on their human families. One of the things that our kind can do is influence animals' minds and make them do their bidding. Like hunting and killing ones that the elders feel are their enemies."

The girl paused for a minute and then took a deep breath, "Today, my grandparents were looking out of the kitchen window and saw that your dog refused to let the two of you cross the street."

Nodding, Alan replied, "Yes. I've never seen that before. It was unusual for Teddy to act that way."

144

"Yes," Yulianna agreed, "A vampire was trying to influence your dog in a bad way but was not able to do so, and it frustrated him. Now he is afraid."

"Whoa!" Piker yelped, "A vampire? And here I was thinking that this was totally a *Saw* kinda thing, but it's actually *Dracula*?"

Piker started spinning around in place, imitating a whirling UFO out of control, "Whooooooooo......!"

"Will you stop that?" screamed Yulianna.

"No!" Piker screamed back, "You stop it! You think we're a couple of idiots? You and your family are not the first to come to Hawaiʻi and try to run a scam on everybody! First, it was bankers and businessmen and then psychics and Tarot cards and car dealers and restaurants, but this takes the cake! Vampires? Gimme a freakin' break. Your Mediterranean Café is a damned good front. I'll give you that! So tell me, how much money do we have to give you so that you can make the Vampire Cullen go away, huh?"

Yulianna grabbed Piker by his orange afro and dragged him to the other side of the sidewalk, where she threw him to the pavement. Piker was too stunned to say anything.

"Don't you ever compare my family to a bunch of wandering nomads or sparkly movie characters! For thousands of years, my clan has allowed common people like yourselves to sleep peacefully at night! You have no idea that you are one step away from being destroyed! Orange părul prost!"

Piker slowly stood up and tried his best to assuage the girl's anger.

"Alright, relax. Be cool," looking at Alan, he continued, "You sure you wanna be her boyfriend?"

"You wanna get your ass kicked some more?" Alan sighed, "Go on, Yulianna."

"When a vampire cannot control an animal or a human being, he or she becomes afraid they will be found out." Looking around at the people passing by, she urged Alan and Piker to continue walking, "So, to prevent that, the vampire will find that animal or human being and kill them."

"So you're saying that Teddy found a vampire?" Alan asked.

"Yes," Yulianna replied, "He didn't just find the vampire. He knows where it is."

"Alright, Teddy!" Piker cheered.

"So, where is it?" Alan said.

Yulianna replied with a fatal resignation, "On the second floor, above our café."

Alexandru confided in Andrei as they sat in the Café while eating Greek olives, "Is your mind clear, Andrei?"

Andrei nodded and continued picking out the darker colored olives from the bowl between the two of them.

"Today, we have let outsiders into our circle. Innocent boys who know nothing of what we do. They will make a good offering for the elder who sleeps above us."

"No," Alexandru said firmly.

"No?" Andrei replied, "You will stand against your own family then?"

"Yes," Alexandru looked at his younger brother in the eyes.

"It is true then. You've killed our kind before," Andrei was stunned at the confirmation.

"Andrei," Alexandru said as he placed a lighter–colored olive into his mouth, "You have perfected the technique of marinating these olives in a jar. The juices seem to explode in your mouth whether you bite into it or just let it sit on your tongue. It is a work of art! The Greeks may have invented everything, but you have them beat with their own olives!"

"You have been one man all by yourself these many years, brother of mine," Andrei began. "Luck has been on your side as you have encountered one elder every few years, but now word will travel back to the homeland and, sooner than you expect, more elders will come. Are you prepared for that, Alexandru?"

"I believe," Alexandru replied, "that the correct technique in marinating a good olive is patience. The perfection of your olives did not happen overnight. It happened over time. Today, your olive making has become second nature to you, and you could more than likely prepare your olives with your eyes closed. Like you, I have also perfected my technique over time. I wouldn't go so far as to say that my technique has become a work of art, but it certainly gets the job done."

Heading toward the back door of the kitchen, Alexandru turned to Andrei and bowed his head, "My respect to you, young brother."

"Wow," Piker sighed.

"So, what's the thrust here? I mean, are you guys gonna get rid of him or what?" Alan asked.

Yulianna put her head down and replied, "It's not that simple."

"I don't understand," Alan said.

"Haven't you been listening to what she's been saying?" Piker interrupted, "Her family is like Renfield from *Dracula*. They are the servants to the vampire that wants to kill Teddy! Geeze, didn't you pay attention to all those horror films we watched in high school?"

"You were actually paying attention to those movies?" Alan was shocked, "I thought we took girls to those horror flicks so that they would scare the crap out themselves and then climb all over us so that we could comfort them?"

"Good god, Higashi, pay attention!" Piker shrieked, "Didn't you hear the part where she mentioned having to FEED the elders? What do you think it is that they were feeding them? Certainly not borscht, I can tell you that much!"

"Is that true?" half-smiling Alan asked Yulianna, "Are you guys gonna feed us to your vampire elder?"

"There is a way out of this," Yulianna replied.

Both Alan and Piker threw their hands up in frustration and let out a huge sigh.

"No, listen!" Yulianna pleaded, "There is a jeweled sword that is used to kill elders like the one we have. Meet me back here after work; we can go upstairs just before the sun sets. When the elder rises from his casket, you can use the jeweled sword that I will give you, and you can kill the elder by chopping his head off, and your dog will be safe as well as the two of you! Be back here after work! I have to get back to the café."

Before she left, Yulianna gave Alan a long passionate kiss and then went on her way.

"You know we're being set up, right? You're not gonna fall for the helpless vampire servant girl thing, right?" Piker asked.

"You still got those two Katana back at the office?" Alan asked Piker.

"Yeah, of course. My dad would kill me if he knew I had 'em. Rumor has it that those two swords were blessed by the Emperor's personal priest in Japan."

"Just in case the jeweled sword doesn't work, it might be nice to have some legit backup. Just in case."

Smiling now, Piker said, "I like the way you think Higashi!"

Teddy wasn't happy to see Kenzie walk into the office and make herself at home at Alan's desk. She began rummaging through his drawers and almost seemed to be disappointed when she didn't find anything incriminating. Leaning back now in Alan's swivel chair, Kenzie saw the taped-up photograph of Kelly Hu on Alan's board and immediately tore it into pieces. She tossed it into the wastebasket that Alan shared with Piker. Kenzie began to rock back and forth in Alan's chair in an almost manic fashion.

Teddy watched her. There was a smell about the woman that Teddy didn't like at all. It was an almost clinical hospital-like smell that gave off the air of death as if it had followed her back from her last stay at the place where humans were not well in their thoughts. He was anxious, also, as he awaited the return of his man. Time was of the essence, and he had already spoken with his mind to the very ones who would help him with what he needed.

Kenzie had no idea that Teddy sat directly behind her as she rocked furiously back and forth in Alan's chair. The dog took a deep breath and let out a loud bark. The sudden noise startled Kenzie so severely that she let out a scream and fell backward out of the chair, and hit her head on the floor. When she looked up and realized that it was Teddy, she could have sworn that the dog had a smile on his face.

Alan and Piker returned to the office and found Kenzie kneeling on the floor as she held her hands on to the back of her head. Teddy was sitting quietly on the floor in front of Alan's desk and quickly got up to greet him and Piker.

"Kenzie," Alan sighed, "You know my boss banned you from this office; if he sees you here, he'll have you arrested, and I'll lose my job!"

"Relax, will you? I just wanted to get my key back from you because I don't have anywhere to stay right now, so you know..." Kenzie trailed off.

"Pssshhh..." Piker blurted out, "Psycho."

"Half-bred, orange Q-tip," Kenzie shot back.

"Oh my god!" Piker screamed, "I've got the perfect come back for that, but you know what? I'm not even gonna go there!"

"Why?" Kenzie replied in her little girl voice, "Because you know I'll kick your ass?"

"You guys," Alan interrupted, "Cut it out before we all get into trouble!"

"No," Piker continued as he completely ignored Alan, "It's because I don't like you. You're not worth the time and energy it takes to even care enough to let your comments have an effect on me to the point where I feel that you even deserve a response! See, Higashi here won't do anything about it because you've convinced him that he is somehow responsible for your screwed-up life, but he's not. This man loathes you, but his heart is too big to kick you out of his place or slam the door shut on you whenever you decide to show up at his doorstep after you've gone out on one of your psychotic binges! Furthermore, I dislike you with such a purple passion that if you even lay a finger on me, I will literally, with my teeth, tear your flesh from limb to limb. It will feel like a complete victory for me to be bathed in your blood because then, and only then, would I know that you were truly dead. Then you would never trouble Higashi's life ever again!"

Piker and Kenzie's faces were mere inches away from one another, teeth bare as if they were wild animals that were on the verge of decimating each other. Just then, Alan happened to glance down at Teddy and saw his dog peek around the outside of the cubicle. As Alan took a quick glance to see what Teddy was looking at, he saw his boss heading straight toward his work area. There was no time to think. Alan grabbed Kenzie by the back of her neck and twisted her arm behind her back. Kenzie let out a painful scream.

"Ow! What the hell, Alan?"

Shouting now at the top of his lungs, Alan manifested a voice from within his gut that he never knew existed. "I TOLD YOU TO NEVER COME BACK HERE, BUT YOU DON'T FRICKIN' LISTEN! FORGET THE DAMNED COPS, KENZIE, I'LL KILL YOU MYSELF THE NEXT TIME I SEE YOU HERE!"

Alan's boss had no time to react to the scene that was unfolding before him. He and Piker were in shock as they watched Alan hurry Kenzie down the stairway, out the door, and into the street. Practically pushing her out into the middle of traffic, Kenzie was nearly hit by a speeding car. Hurrying back onto the sidewalk, she was just able to see Alan mouth the word "sorry" as he locked the door in front of her.

Bounding back up the stairs, Alan returned to find his boss with Piker and Teddy in his cubicle.

"Boss, I'm sorry," Alan began to explain.

"No, no," Alan's boss replied, "You handled that really well! I'm the one that has to apologize. I took you for somebody who would cave into someone like Kenzie, I mean, she can be quite persuasive, but you stood your ground. Good for you, Alan, good for you!"

"Was there something you needed us to do, boss?" Alan asked.

"Oh, yes!" his boss replied, "I have a business meeting that's going to run a little late into the evening, so I won't be back tonight. There's a report that's coming in from New York via fax. I need you to monitor the fax. You need to make sure it prints out in full form with no interruptions. For some reason, they don't want to email it. I don't know how long these printouts will take, but I need them for a conference call first thing tomorrow. Alan, you and Piker put your selves down for overtime, okay?"

"Sure thing, boss," Alan replied.

"Thanks, boss, we're on it!" Piker called out.

"Alright!" the boss replied, "Just close up everything after you get done in here. See you guys in the morning!"

As soon as their boss was out of sight, Piker gave Alan a nudge on his shoulder, "Man, what got into you? I was ready to pound Kenzie, and you just jumped in like psycho Al Pacino!" Piker laughed.

"I was not about to get us fired over her drama, so I did the only thing I could think of," Alan said almost sheepishly.

"Alright, well, let's get our own work done so that we don't have to do it tomorrow."

Sitting down in his swivel chair, Alan immediately noticed that his picture of Kelly Hu was gone. He quickly around his desk until he finally saw that what was left of the image was in his wastebasket. It was torn to shreds.

"Fucking psycho! I should have pushed her in front of a truck!" Alan cursed to himself.

It was six 'o clock in the evening. The sun had already set behind the west Waiʻanae mountains. Alan and Piker stood near the fax machine eating a pizza that they had ordered from a mom–and–pop pizzeria a block away from their office. The almost mechanical droning of the papers spewing themselves out in metronome timing began to have a hypnotic effect on the two young men. They began to get tired and almost lethargic.

"This pizza is too heavy on the sausage and garlic. It's awful for us. I can feel my arteries hardening," Alan said.

"No more than I can feel myself getting varicose veins in my face," Piker added.

"More Monster?" Alan asked.

"Oh, god, please! Yes!" Piker nodded.

"Green or blue?"

"Borg blue for me!"

"That leaves *Matrix* green for me!" Alan laughed.

Piker suddenly began to giggle and said, "I can't believe we're getting paid to do this!"

"Well," Alan countered, "It could very well be that he might have asked everyone else in the office to do the same thing, and they all refused. Maybe we were his last choice?"

"Even if that was the case," Piker said, "He may very well be appreciative of the fact that we didn't say no even though everyone else did."

"You're the yin to my yang Piker Teruya," Alan laughed.

"Is that the white part or the black part? I always forget," Piker asked.

The moment was broken by the sound of Teddy's deep, low growl as it came from their cubicle down the hallway. Looking at one another, they both walked briskly back to their office space to see what it was that got Teddy upset.

They found Teddy at the top of the landing, which led to a staircase leading down toward the street, the same staircase that Alan used to usher Kenzie out of the building.

Kneeling down to pet Teddy's back, Alan asked, "What's wrong, Teddy? Everything okay?"

"Higashi," Piker said, "I think we forgot about our meeting with your friend. Her entire family is here."

Yulianna stood at the bottom of the staircase with her family gathered around her. Just behind the group, standing in the shadows was a taller, more refined–looking man who was clean–cut and well–groomed. He wore a grayish–green suit with a scarf about his neck, and his eyes were piercing and very powerful.

Teddy became more and more agitated, and his growl became deeper and guttural until it almost sounded human. It caught Piker's attention and, even before he knew what it was he said, it had already come out of his mouth without a second thought.

"There is no invitation to be had in this place. None of you are welcome here. Leave!"

Looking at Piker now, Alan quickly retrieved the two Katana out from under Piker's desk and handed one to his friend.

"You heard him," Alan said, "No invite. No entrance."

The tall figure stepped forward as his family members moved aside for him, "Scuze, we mean no offense. However, as you have already been told by my great–great–great–great grandchild, Yulianna, I need your canine. Ma invita, invite me in, and I will take the animal and be gone."

"This is not only *Saw* but its *Misery* too..." Piker whispered.

"No," Alan insisted, "It's *Wrong Turn*, but it's vampires instead of inbred, cannibal rednecks."

"Please," the stranger's voice echoed from the bottom of the staircase, "An invitation. We will take what we need and be gone."

Teddy stepped forward as his growl became maniacal while Alan and Piker replied with a firm, "NO!"

"Ah!" the figure laughed, "The predictability of human nature always gives itself away, and the feeble mind is always ready to be molded. I anticipated your resistance to my demands and, so, I came prepared."

Opening the door that led out to the street, the figure gestured to someone who stood outside and waved that person in. It was someone that the figure took into his embrace intimately and kissed on the forehead. It was Kenzie.

"Go to the top of the stairs, my love, and give us our invitation," the figure instructed.

Kenzie slowly made her way up the stairs, dramatically taking each step one by one. Alan's heart sank as he realized that Kenzie must have fallen under the influence of the figure.

Alan's grip on the Katana handle intensified as the years of training he received were now coming to the fore. The only weakness he possessed was what he still felt in his heart for Kenzie and, yes, that sense of being responsible for the way her life turned out. He couldn't even muster the words necessary to stop her slow but deliberate climb up the stairs. With each step, Kenzie's smile grew broader and more malicious, and it began to reveal her fangs that were now slowly growing out.

"I asked the elder to let me kill you first, Alan, after I extended the invitation to my new family because you're weak. I know in your heart that the best thing you could have done all these years was to rid yourself of me, and then your life would return to normal. I knew that was the right thing to do. I knew that I sucked the joy out of your life and made you miserable, but I was too selfish to care. I purposely created drama in your life so that I could keep you with me. Now, as soon as I am within arm's reach of your wretched form, I am going to literally suck the life out of you," Kenzie said.

"Look at you," she continued, "stuck for words like always. Here you are at the crucial moment when you should do the right thing that would better your life and you can't. That's why I want to kill you, Alan, because you're so easy to manipulate and, no matter what it is that I do to you, you'll just stand there and take it up the ass with no resistance."

With Kenzie standing just two steps below him, she leaned forward and said, "Boo!"

In the blink of an eye, Alan withdrew the blessed Katana from its sheath with his right hand and, at the same time, pulled the sheath away with his left hand. His left hip snapped back, bringing his body into a horse stance. As the sword flew out of its home, it cut down at an arc from a high left angle and swept down toward the right, thus quickly and cleanly decapitating Kenzie's head from her body.

The motion was so swift that it took a second before anyone realized what had happened, particularly Kenzie herself. She could not comprehend the circumstances until the moment that her head landed perfectly on the very bottom step. It was only then that she saw her own headless form tumbling down the stairs toward her.

160

Using his sleeve to wipe the blood from the blade, Alan sheathed his Katana and let out a long slow breath.

"I was wrong," Alan said, "I'm not sorry."

"Guess we don't need a jeweled sword after all, huh, Higashi?" Piker said as he readied himself for whatever was about to happen.

He didn't have to wait long. The figure let out a loud roar and flew up the stairs with a blood-red rage that filled his eyes. Teddy leaped forward and stood on his hind legs as he put himself between the two men and the figure.

In an instant, the retriever turned into an eight-foot-tall Hawaiian man dressed in a rust-colored malo who stood there and met the figure's attack head-on. His skin was a dark brown, and he wore a full beard and had wild, gabardine-like hair. Grabbing the figure by the throat with one hand, the Hawaiian man crushed its neck and began to thrash the body about as if the figure himself was nothing but a mere rag doll. With no fight left in the body of the vampire, the Hawaiian man used his bare hands to snap the figure's head away and threw everything he held in his hands back down the stairs. Yulianna and her family ran screaming out the door and into the dark night, horrified at what they had just witnessed.

"Holy crap!" Piker said, "I I don't even have a movie reference for this!"

"Teddy?" Alan asked hesitantly.

The huge man stood there with lean muscles rippling beneath his skin. He shook his head in response to Alan's question and answered, "Kaupe."

"I gave you those boys and the dog on a silver platter! Solely as a consolidation that you would all get the job done, I let the elder turn Alan's girlfriend into one of us, but what happened? Tell me what happened! I purposely made them stay back at the office to be sitting ducks, and what happened? What went wrong?" Dennis Iordache screamed. His voice boomed like a million bolts of lightning, and it began to cause the ears of Andrei and his family to bleed.

"We have never been to your office before tonight, father, so we were therefore bound by the protocol of invitation," Andrei said. Watching his entire family cower in fear as they all stood before the father vampire, Andrei realized how correct his older brother Alexandru might be.

Andrei now longed for the chilled air from his homeland in Transylvania. There seemed to be a kind of magic in the air during that time of year. It always reminded him of being a child again when the world seemed free and without trouble. How he wished it were so at this very moment. For the first time in many years, Andrei's heart began to fill itself with a warmth that he believed was long gone. A man must nearly have no soul within himself to live the kind of life that he has and had subjected his family to as well. Yet here it was, tears flowing freely from not only his eyes but his very being. He realized that there was some semblance of humanity within him. He would give anything to protect them.

"The fault is mine, father," Andrei said humbly, "I was present, and if there is anyone who should suffer for the death of the elder, then it should be me."

With his eyes now gleaming blood–red and with his fangs bare, Dennis Iordache responded, "I am glad you agree. You are responsible, and you will pay with your life while your family watches you die!"

His tone of voice becoming much sweeter, Dennis Iordache continued, "And when I am done with you, I will kill what remains of your family."

"Father, is there no honor left amongst our kind? Are we completely animalistic? I beg you not to make my family suffer for the transgression that is mine!" Andrei pleaded.

"Do not beg, brother. It ill becomes you to do so," the voice came from the back of the room.

It was Alexandru who now had Teddy, Alan, and Piker behind him. A second later, two more dogs appeared; a pit bull and a Rottweiler along with a massive black pig. All four animals suddenly took the form of Hawaiian men who were all eight feet tall and well-muscled. Their eyes glowed blue as they stood there, dressed only in their malo.

"Alan, Piker. Take my brother and his family and leave. We have business to conduct with the father. Go now," Alexandru instructed.

Without hesitation, the young men safely conducted Andrei and his family out of the empty room and into a waiting van that would take them to a house on the windward side of the island.

"I can't believe it," Piker said, shaking his head.

"What?" Alan asked.

"I have no movie reference for this situation!" Piker screeched.

"That's because we're living the movie of our lives, Piker. Believe me, despite everything that's happened, there is going to be a happy ending with no sequel because life after this will be what we make it," Alan said.

"That's deep, Higashi. That's really deep," Piker began to choke up.

"So," Dennis Iordache said, "You've brought yourself and four animals to kill me? Three dog men, I can understand but a pig as well?"

"These are neither dog men nor a pig; these are Hawaiian Gods. The retriever is Kaupe, this pit bull is Poki and that Rottweiler is Kuʻilioloa. The pig you scoff at is Kamapuaʻa."

"Thus, my question, is it going to take all of you just to kill me?" Dennis Iordache asked.

"No," Alexandru replied, "It will take only me to do it."

"So confident you are but then, why the Hawaiian Gods? Have you become one of those strange humans who requires an audience to perform?" Dennis Iordache mocked Alexandru now.

"No," Alexandru continued. "They are here as witnesses. Until tonight they have been told to stay away from the affairs of men and not to interfere. I need them to see the kind of vile wretchedness that your kind may bring to these islands should your disease ever spread itself amongst us. It would be many times worse than any epidemic they've yet known."

"I like your resolve. It's refreshing! But it has also made you overly confident. You don't really think that you can kill me all by yourself? Do you?"

"When I was a younger man, I had no problem whatsoever when I took the head of your older brother Decebal. The same way that I am going to take yours," Alexandru smiled.

Dennis Iordache roared like an animal as the windows shattered all around him. Alexandru withdrew the jeweled sword from his coat without hesitation. He awaited the onslaught of the father vampire, but it never came. In a second, Dennis Iordache was gone as he took the form of a giant bat and flew toward Honolulu Harbor just past the Aloha Tower.

"He's getting away!" Alexandru shouted.

"Mai hopohopo," the voice spoke in Alexandru's head. It was Kaupe.

"Not to worry," Kaupe continued, "There is help. Through my report to my fellow brethren, we have paid witness to the truth. He will not escape."

The father vampire's animal form was inundated by an army of pueo who scratched and pulled him straight into the waters of Mamala at Honolulu harbor. The pueo then flew off into the night while the creature was forced to return to its human form.

Dennis Iordache came to the surface to see another tall Hawaiian man dressed in a red malo standing at the end of the pier just at the back of the Aloha Tower. The shape of his white hair bunched up at the top of his head seemed to resemble a fin. His white beard seemed to glow against his dark skin as his eyes shown blue. His hands were tattooed, and his body was more massive than the other Hawaiian gods he saw previously.

In a second, the Hawaiian man dove effortlessly into the water without a splash. Before Dennis Iordache knew what was happening, the biggest shark he had ever seen burst to the surface and scooped him up in his mouth. It tightened his teeth around his body so that no amount of otherworldly strength could loosen it.

The shark now swam back towards the pier where Dennis Iordache now saw Alexandru standing at the edge of the dock amongst his godly companions. In his hand, he held the jeweled sword. The mighty shark dove quickly underwater and went deeper and deeper into the dark waters in the harbor. The underwater pressure began to be too much for the father vampire, who let out a scream that no one could hear as the saltwater started to fill his lungs. Suddenly, the shark's direction changed, and he was now heading straight toward the surface. His form burst through the water with the father vampire still in the grip of his massive razor-sharp teeth. He emerged close enough to the edge of the pier that Alexandru could now reach out with a stroke of his jeweled sword and sever Dennis Iordache's head from his body. His other hand grabbed the dirty blonde hair of the father vampire at the same time.

With the monstrous shark now slipping back into the deep, he made a quick meal of the two hundred–year–old body that became as nothing in his mouth. With his duty done, he swam silently away toward his home just beneath the sacred heiau on Hawaiʻi Island known as Puʻukohola.

"Kamohoaliʻi!" Alexandru called out, "Mahalo piha nui ia ʻoe e ke akua!"

Tucking the head of the father vampire in his coat, Alexandru quickly dried it off and then began to douse it with lighter fluid and set it on fire. When he turned to thank the other gods, they were gone. Quickly making his way back up to Bishop Street, Alexandru got in his car. He needed to get back to his house, where he was sure that Andrei, his family, and the two young men were waiting.

The drive through the night toward the Pali tunnel filled Alexandru's thought with one wish, and that was to get home. Going into the tunnel itself and then emerging on the Koʻolau side of the island was like being cleansed every time. The fragrance of fresh rain or that of the ocean as the wind carried that smell toward the mountains constantly reminded Alexandru of what was most important in his life. It made him smile with tears of joy whenever he thought of it.

A short time later, as he pulled his car into the driveway of his Hamakua Street home, he was greeted by shrill screams of joy. This was more precious than any diamond, sapphire, or ruby that decorated his ancient jeweled sword. It was the laughter of his grandchildren who climbed all over him as he knelt down to greet them.

"Papa! Papa! Papa!"

Carrying them all into the house, he was greeted by his eldest daughter, Pua. She pulled all of her children off of their grandfather and made them all go back into their bedroom to sleep because it was so late. He was then greeted by his wife, Melia, who told him that Andrei and his family were sitting out in the backyard. Alan, Piker, and Alexandru's son-in-law, Pua's husband, La'akea, were preparing steaks on the hibachi for them to enjoy. Taking in a deep breath and slowly letting it out, Alexandru was happy to see them all safe and sound. Just then, Andrei came up and hugged his brother and let loose a flood of tears.

"I now understand why this place and these people are so important to you. You have a family of your own, children and grandchildren just like I do. Tonight I was willing to die for them, and now that I am here, I see your reasons why you do what you do. I am proud of you, brother, and I support you should trouble ever arise again. But I have to ask you, who were those large Hawaiian men, and where did those other animals come from?"

As Andrei went on with his questions, Alexandru saw the golden retriever sitting just near the place where Alan had made a seat for himself. The two made eye contact as the retriever nodded in his direction. Alexandru returned a wink and a nod as well. The stars seemed to be like clusters as there were no clouds in the sky. Manaiakalani, Maui's magic fishhook, was clear to see that night. That alone was a good sign indeed.

In the ensuing years of Decebal's death, Alexandru began to suspect that the elders had an inside connection to Hawai'i somehow. Alexandru knew that there were no families from the old country in the islands at the time that could host and feed an elder without being found out. Therefore, the contact had to be a singular source.

Alexandru was fortunate to have found work as a Stevedore and began to also monitor the import and export business near the waterfront for any indication of who it might be. Bringing in an elder by air freight was too risky, so it had to be done by ship. There were no clues anywhere until fourteen years ago in 1999 when a man named Iordache opened a small import/export exchange. It sat on the corner of Queen and Alakea Streets.

It was a curious move considering that the corner of Queen and Alakea had a reputation among the better

Hawaiian populace as being a home of restless spirits. Every local business person knew that that two–story building was haunted and refused to open an office there. Alexandru knew that only one without roots in the islands would start a business in that location. So he watched the building closely for many years. One day, Alexandru saw that two new, young, local boys had been hired, and he immediately tried to think of an idea as to how those two boys could be his eyes in that office.

By this time in his life, Alexandru was already well versed in akua and 'aumakua due to his Hawaiian wife's influence. Through her, he discovered that some ceremonies that people thought were no longer practiced were still prevalent in Melia's family.

One evening, his wife said to him as casual as you please, "Would you like to meet one of the Akua? In some circles, he is considered a kupua as well, but his mana is still the same."

Without a second thought, Alexandru agreed. A short time later, in the dead of night, he found himself in the passenger seat of their car as they drove to the Pali Lookout. As the pair made their way past the lookout, they headed down the old access road that brought many travelers to the Windward side of 'O'ahu. The couple took two flashlights with them and only managed to get twenty feet down the road when they suddenly came upon a brindled dog.

Alexandru's wife began to address the animal in Hawaiian, and, to his surprise, the dog responded as if he knew exactly what it was that Melia was saying. She then pointed to Alexandru, and the dog walked right up to him. In the blink of an eye, the dog transformed himself into an eight-foot-tall Hawaiian man. He was muscular and resembled the classic Hawaiian images of warriors Alexandru had seen in so many lithographs and paintings. However, the thought came to Alexandru; elder vampires were one thing but a Hawaiian werewolf?

Melia introduced the fabled Akua 'Īlio as Kaupe. He had gained a reputation as a consumer of innocents. Yet here he was extending his hand in friendship in order to help Alexandru up. Melia told him that Kaupe was a guardian of her family for centuries, as were many other akua, kupua and 'aumakua.

Melia explained to Kaupe what her husband did and his concern regarding the potential spread of vampires in the islands. Although the gods were not to interfere in men's affairs until the proper time had come, Kaupe agreed to lend his assistance to help Alexandru's plight. After all, they were dealing with other-worldly creatures, not men.

On the weekend at their iaido practice, Alan and Piker were goofing off with a real katana. Alan accidentally cut Piker on his forearm, requiring a trip to the Straub Emergency room, where Piker got fifteen stitches. Alexandru watched Alan during that whole scenario. He followed Alan to the emergency room to observe. As Alan stood outside on Hotel Street and Ward, Kaupe appeared and mimicked the form of a golden retriever puppy that walked up to Alan and won his heart over. Alan named the dog Teddy after his favorite local 70's singer Teddy Rendazo.

Kaupe would share information with Alexandru for two years without incident, until the day that Alexandru's own family elder turned up. It was purely a coincidence that his brother's café opened only a block up from the import/export office. However, when Kaupe relayed to Alexandru the incident concerning the elder's telepathic communication, everything began to fall into place.

Andrei and his family picked up the old crate while Alexandru was with his wife's family. The elder, much to Alexandru's benefit, was ancient and very arrogant. As it is with most vampire lore, the one who lay in a casket in the empty room above the café began to put out his powers to see who and what it was that he could start to influence. His ego was immediately challenged once he realized that he could not control Teddy or, rather, Kaupe at all. He unknowingly exposed himself once he began to communicate with Kaupe.

When Alan and Piker took the retriever back to the office, the dog had every intention of following them back to the café. At that moment, Kaupe latched on to another telepathic communication between the elder from the café to someone in Alan's office.

It turned out to be Alan and Piker's boss, Dennis. Thus, the plan of action was put forward by Alexandru and Kaupe. Dennis Iordache had done a meticulously good job of not being found out. He was smart to not let the arrival and misdeeds of previous elders who had come to the islands be traced back to him.

With the arrival of the new elder, Dennis made himself known to Andrei. He had counted on Andrei's obedience but had not anticipated Andrei's dogmatic adherence to ancient tradition. Dennis intended to offer the two young men to the elder as a pact of sorts to gain his cooperation.

The turning of Kenzie into a newborn was an extra safety precaution that Dennis Iordache had to take. He had intercepted Kenzie just as she was rounding the corner at South King and Richard Streets and immediately apologized to her for what transpired in his office. He told her that he had changed his mind and would allow her to come to the exchange of her own free will. Unprepared for Dennis's kindness, Kenzie did the only thing she could think of, and that was to give him a hug. It was at that moment that the father vampire quickly bit Kenzie and held her tight. Although people walking by could see the two in an intimate embrace, they ignored their public display of affection and went about their business. The two had little clue that this day would be the beginning of the end.

Later that evening, as Andrei and his family fled the exchange office, Alexandru appeared with his kino lau cohorts in tow. As much as possible, with as little time that they had left, he and Kaupe explained everything to Alan and Piker.

The evening ended late as everyone had already gone off to sleep one by one. The only ones left still sitting near the hibachi with a beer in their hands and small remnants of teriyaki beef on a paper plate were Alexandru, Alan, and Piker. They sat there and watched the stars above them from the backyard of Papa Dru's Kaʻelepulu home.

"So the gods have your back?" Alan asked.

"Correction," Alexandru replied, "The gods have my wife's back. She is Hawaiian; I am not. I do not assume to be Hawaiian by marriage. I know my place in the order of things among the pantheon of gods here in this land. I will say confidently that I love my wife and my children and grandchildren. I will move heaven and earth to protect them from harm. I have and will continue to do so. Based on that and with the love of my wife, the gods have given me favor. I am humbled by it."

"What do we do now?" Piker asked, "We don't have a job anymore."

"Well," Alexandru said, "I know a few things about the import/export business, and I am sure I can step in to fill that duty right away. However, I may need two supervisors to oversee daily operational procedures. What say you?"

"I say yes," Alan said.

"Yes, for me," Piker agreed.

"Hiki no," Kaupe chimed in. The unexpected reply made Alan and Piker jump out of their chairs.

"Is he going to be doing that a lot?" Alan asked.

"No," Alexandru replied, "He'll go back to being Kaupe who roams the Nu'uanu Pali area, or he can do as he pleases."

Just then, Yulianna appeared at the back door of her great uncle's house and was staring intently at Alan.

"I think she wants to have a word with you," Alexandru insisted.

"Uh, I don't know. I mean, after all, she did try to feed me to her elder," Alan said.

"She had no choice at the time, Alan. She was bound by the restraints of an old tradition that does not have a place in Hawai'i. She knows that now and tonight, she was liberated from those bonds. Go and talk to her. We will be here when you return," Alexandru was warm and encouraging as Alan rose from his chair and made his way to where Yulianna now waited.

Taking another sip of his beer, Alexandru leaned across and earnestly asked Piker, "Tell me something. How did you get that orange hair?"

AFTERWORD

The character of Alexandru is based on a man named Adnan Bin Abulkareem Ahmed Al-Kaissy El Farthie. When I first met him in 1988, he stood across the wrestling ring from me dressed in a Native American war bonnet, and his name was Chief Billy White Wolf. Like Alexandru's character in the story, I was still new to the business. I would spend the early part of my career doing the job for the more experienced guys in the industry. On that particular night, neither my opponent nor Adnan's opponent showed up for the card. The lineup needed a last-minute shuffle, and so referee Sammy Samson came into the heel locker room and gave me the news.

"Your opponent made a no show," he said, "And Billy's match didn't show either, so Lars said to tell you that you're gonna work with Billy. The old man is tired, and he wants to go home, so as soon the bell rings, you blindside him and beat the shit out of him for a minute, then let him make his comeback. He's gonna shoot you into the ropes and give you the double tomahawk chop, you sell his finish and lay down, and Billy gets the three count, and we all go home, okay?"

"Okay," I said.

It ended up being one of the best matches in my entire professional wrestling career. I had great respect for the man, and I thought he and I would have a program together, but it never worked out. Imagine my surprise when I found out that Chief Billy White Wolf wasn't even Native American! He is Armenian from the Middle East. Turns out that his old high school classmate was Saddam Hussein, but that's another story.

So when these stories came to me, the face of Alexandru was the face of Adnan. In my mind, there was no other person who could be the basis for this character. I meant to go into greater detail as to Alexandru's background before arriving here in our pae 'aina. There was a whole section that described his escape from Soviet–occupied Romania in 1944. Sometimes, as many an actor has said, less is more. The important thing was that I knew Alexandru's story. That is the source from which I drew my inspiration for this man's lifelong mission. As for Adnan, where ever you are, my friend, I hope you are safe and well and that perhaps we may cross paths again, but under more agreeable circumstances.

Mahalo.

About the Author

Lopaka Kapanui is a native Hawaiian storyteller, author, actor, kumu hula, cultural practitioner, former professional wrestler, husband, father and grandpa. Sometimes known as "The Ghost Guy," Lopaka makes a business of leading guests into some of the darkest, spookiest places on the island of ʻOʻahu.

His family's legends, history, customs and protocol were passed down to Lopaka in the traditional Hawaiian way, through moʻolelo, from mouth to ear, sitting at the feet of his Mom and his Aunty as they related the lessons to him. He learned of the night marchers who only appeared during a particular moon phase. He learned why it is important to never share food with anyone while walking through a haunted place. He also learned the significance of the proper prayers to offer in ceremonial blessings, to enter or leave a sacred place, to ask for protection or forgiveness, or before gathering greenery in depths of a Hawaiian forest, and the importance of intent. Additionally, he was taught that the responsibility which would come with what he was going to inherit would have to, one day, be passed down within his own family.

In March 1994, Lopaka followed a friend's recommendation and went on a ghost tour with famed historian and author of "Obake Files" and the "Chicken Skin" ghost story series, Glen Grant. At the time, he had no idea that he was about to meet his future mentor. Lopaka quickly realized that the stories that Glen told were the same tales of legends and history that his own kupuna shared with him.

Glen was adamant about researching every story, every fact and instilled this ethic in Lopaka as well, accepting nothing less than excellence. After Glen's passing in 2003, Lopaka carried on the business at The Haunt for a short time and then created his own tour business, first as Ghosts of Old Honolulu as a tribute to Glen and then Mysteries of Honolulu. It is through Mysteries of Honolulu that Lopaka followed in the footsteps of his close friend and mentor and honors the man who meant so much to him.

Inspired by Glen's constant encouragement to do more and be more, Lopaka began chronicling the supernatural experiences of himself and others. His business transitioned into Mysteries of Hawai'i, expanding his storytelling and tours to the neighbor islands, encompassing the legends and mystery of this island state.

Having been in the storytelling business for more than 20 years, hundreds of people have come forward to share their own stories with Lopaka as well, making him a repository of sorts for some of our islands' spookiest tales.

Made in the USA
Columbia, SC
20 October 2024

44374016R00107